MURDER MACHREE

"In this subtly compelling good-twin/bad-twin story, Boylan writes with such credibility that readers will suspect her characters of existence beyond the pages of her book. . . . [MURDER MACHREE] will engross even the most demanding readers."
—*Publishers Weekly*

MURDER OBSERVED

"An intricate, multifaceted puzzle . . . There's wit and warmth here, and even some wisdom. It's a little as if Jane Austen had turned to detection."
—*The Philadelphia Inquirer*

WORKING MURDER

"Boylan has created a terse, old-fashioned mystery, sprinkled with humor and urbanity in the manner of Christie."
—*Pittsburgh Post-Gazette*

By Eleanor Boylan
Published by Ivy Books:

WORKING MURDER
MURDER OBSERVED
MURDER MACHREE
PUSHING MURDER

PUSHING
MURDER

Eleanor Boylan

IVY BOOKS • NEW YORK

Ivy Books
Published by Ballantine Books
Copyright © 1993 by Eleanor Boylan

Library of Congress Catalog Card Number: 93-15156

ISBN 0-8041-1251-7

This edition published by arrangement with Henry Holt and Company, Inc.

Manufactured in the United States of America

First Ballantine Books Edition: January 1995

10 9 8 7 6 5 4 3 2

1

"I COULD NOT BELIEVE, CLARA, THAT YOU'D be so inconsiderate as to die before this matter is settled."

The voice was the voice of my cousin, Charles Saddlier, but Sadd lived in Florida, and I was in bed in New York City trying to get some sleep. And what "matter" was he talking about?

The second voice made even less sense. "You gave us a scare, Mom."

That was my daughter, Paula. But she lived in Boston. *Scare?*

The third voice made the least sense of all. It was female and unknown to me. "Better let her get some sleep."

Thanks, whoever you are. Sleep was all I wanted now, especially as the weird sensation in my stomach was beginning to recede. . . . But why was something pinning my left foot to the bed?

"It was arsenic, Mrs. Gamadge. Do you feel like talking about it?"

Not really. Nor was I at all sure what the attractive, fortyish woman in the white coat meant by "it" unless she was referring to the cast on my ankle, which I'd been told was broken, and what did that have to do with arsenic? I felt miserably confused, but with my family sitting there looking at me expectantly I supposed I must gather my wits.

I'd been told it was ten hours since their voices and that of Dr. Martha Somebody had penetrated my consciousness, that I was in Room 220 at St. Victor's Hospital on Tenth Street, and that "my condition" would keep me there another four or five days. Now pale morning sun slanted through the window, and sitting up in bed in a bright pink bed jacket I'd never seen before, Paula braiding my long white hair which must be in hideous disarray, I felt weak and embarrassed.

I said lamely, "I'm afraid I don't remember much," and looked at Sadd, who was reading, then at my son, Henry, then at his wife, Tina. Their constant presence along with Paula's I'd been dimly feeling. Idiotically I began to cry.

"Go home all of you," I blubbered. "You'll lose your jobs because of me. You haven't left this room for—"

They began telling me to shut up, that now that I was out of danger yes, they'd go about their business, and Sadd, who is my senior by several years and hates New York in the winter, said I didn't seem very grateful that he'd come all the way from Florida when he heard the awful news.

"What awful news?" I was making an earnest effort to put all this together.

2

"That you'd been poisoned, Mom," said Henry gently.

Poisoned? I'd been *poisoned*?

"I came at once," said Sadd, looking virtuous. "And in this appalling December weather too."

Still at sea, I blew him a feeble kiss, and he blew one back. The doctor—I assumed that's what she was—smiled at these family pyrotechnics and said, "Mrs. Gamadge, I'm sorry to press, but if you could remember—"

"Doctor," I said, trying to rally, "I should be the sorry one. You must be a busy woman. Tell me your name."

"Martha Cullen. Your own doctor—Arthur Kingman, isn't it?—is in Bermuda, we learned."

Henry said, "Dr. Cullen was on duty in Emergency when you were brought in, Mom."

Brought in? Brought in from where? From where I'd been poisoned? Broken my ankle? What possible connection could one have with the other—or either one with me, for that matter?

"Let me think . . ." I sat up straighter in the bed and received a twinge in my leg that made me gasp.

Tina, my petite, sensitive daughter-in-law, said at once, "You're not up to this, Clara."

"Yes, I am." I gritted my teeth, a painful act in itself as nothing in my miserable old frame was prime for gritting.

Paula finished my braid and patted the end where she'd attached a little bow. She said, "There. Now you'll be more comfortable. How does she look?"

"Rather like an over-the-hill Rapunzel," Sadd said.

3

This produced giggles from my children, and Dr. Cullen looked a bit aghast, but how could she know my nutty family?

"Doctor, I think it's coming back to me," I said. It was, actually, mistily and piecemeal. "I seem to recall . . ." Then a quick, penetrating ray. "I was lying on a sidewalk somewhere."

Five heads nodded encouragingly, and Henry said, "Cornelia Street, outside your friend's bookstore."

"Bookstore?"

"Sal's new one," said Tina. "The one you thought up a name for?"

"Name?"

I sounded like a darned parrot, but each word I repeated helped to dispel the mist. "Yes, Sal's new store." Then a fine, productive burst. "It was the day she opened!"

Five more vigorous nods, and I waxed positively chatty. "You see, Doctor, this friend of mine has always wanted to open a bookstore specializing in mystery fiction. There are quite a few of them around the country—a famous one here in New York called The Mysterious Bookshop and one in San Diego called Grounds for Murder, and there's Murder Under Cover and The Scene of the Crime—so for my friend's store I came up with Pushing Murder."

I beamed at the doctor, expecting her to be impressed with the cleverness of it, but she looked rather blank.

Paula said loyally, "An inspired name, really."

Henry and Tina agreed that it was, and Sadd, the eternal grammarian, said, "Of course a participle is never as strong as a verb, but in this case it's quite effective."

Dr. Cullen cleared her throat. "Mrs. Gamadge, do you remember whom you talked to and what you ate at that party?"

"Party?" I was feeling spent. I yanked at the bed jacket and tried to concentrate. "Party. Oh, yes. Sal had a wine-and-cheese do. She wasn't really ready to open yet, but with Christmas coming . . ." Oh, no! Christmas—and me in the hospital! I plowed on. "I remember that Sal's husband was still putting up shelves. They've just been married, you know. He's a dear— very handy, too. He made a clever sign for out front. It has the words *Pushing Murder* between bookends that look like tombstones with—"

"Clara," said Sadd, his eyes on his book, "you're rambling."

"I know it." I suddenly felt exhausted, angry, and put upon. "What happened to my ankle, for heaven's sake? It's hurting again."

Dr. Cullen nodded quickly to Paula, who scooted out the door.

Henry said, "What happened was this: You tripped— you were sick as hell—coming down the steps of Sal's store and crashed on the pavement. By the time the paramedics got there you'd passed out. The broken ankle was obvious, but we couldn't figure out why all the puking. Dr. Cullen recognized poisoning and gave you—what's it called, Doctor?"

"Chelation therapy. It's an intravenous treatment."

"So she saved your life, and all we want you to do is tell us who you think might have wanted to take it."

I looked at my son stupidly. "You mean kill me?"

"What else?"

I stared around in bafflement for a few seconds, then felt sudden relief. The answer was obvious.

Sister Agnes, a brisk, sixtyish nun—the floor supervisor, hadn't she told me?—came purposefully into the room. I pushed up the fluffy sleeve of the bed jacket and said, "Dears—and this means you too, Doctor—isn't it perfectly plain what happened? The poison was meant for another person. I simply got the wrong canapé. Somebody who has it in for somebody decided—oh, how sordid and sick!—to do it at Sal's party but did it clumsily and goofed and got me instead. Oh, thank you, Sister!"

The needle was in and out. I closed my eyes and started to count backward. "... Ninety-eight, ninety-seven ... Go home, all of you. I love you ... Don't worry ... Nobody wants to do in poor old Clara ... Ninety-three, ninety-two ... Problem is I love anchovies ... Eighty-eight ... eighty-seven ... eighty-six ... Just want to know one thing ... Sixty ... Fifty ... Where did this awful bed jacket come from? ... Forty-two ... buckle my shoe ..."

"Sal," said Tina's voice.

"What about her? ... Thirty ... Twenty ... Jack jump over the ..."

"She brought the bed jacket."

"Oh ... Fleece was white as ... Eighteen ... Poor Sal ... probably blaming herself ... Shouldn't ...

Ten—no, nine . . . Jack Sprat could eat no . . . I should have been like Jack . . ."

I snickered at this witticism, then felt irritated because they were all still standing there. I'd told them to go. I'd explained everything. Why were they gawking at me and not going?

Well, then, I'd go myself.

I went.

2

I SWAM UP FROM THE DEPTHS OF THE DRUG reluctantly, relaxed, remembering Caliban's words "and when I waked I cried to dream again."

The sun seemed less bright, and there was frost on the window. From somewhere—the street probably—came faint, mechanical strains of "Hark! The Herald Angels Sing."

My eyes focused slowly and showed me Sadd sitting in a chair by the window. My children appeared to have left, thank heaven. Why didn't this dear man go too? I was in no danger; there was no reason for this kind of hospital vigil so wearisome to a family. Sadd had to be exhausted. But oddly, he wasn't even dozing. He was sitting upright, gazing into space. I looked at him over the mound of pillows that supported my knees and tried to figure out what was wrong with this picture. His appearance was no different from what it had been last March when I visited him in Florida. There was no thinning of the heavy white hair, no increased stoop of the shoulders. The different factor was something . . . abstract.

8

My cousin Sadd, you must understand, is an incessant reader. A former publisher, he read, until his retirement, for both business and pleasure, and since then entirely and addictively for pleasure. He claims that if a day goes by without a glimpse of the printed word, he suffers withdrawal pangs. Sadd reads anywhere and everywhere. He reads in the bathroom, in the car, at meals, at parties, sometimes all night, often while sitting before the television, and he always brings a book to church, declaring it's the only way he can survive the sermon. I cannot imagine a place or occasion that would find him without something to read. Sadd will bring a book to Judgment Day.

He was without one now.

I lay considering this phenomenon, then said, "What time is it?"

He got up and came to the bed. "One o'clock. Your lunch tray came and went."

"Not hungry. My stomach still hurts."

"A nurse came in with a pill for that while you were under." Sadd pulled a chair to the bed. "Also the doctor who set your ankle. They'll both be back. How do you feel generally?"

"Somewhat better." I struggled to a sitting position. "Sadd, you have got to get some rest. Where are you staying?"

"Leave out *got*. *Have to* get some rest. Henry and Tina insisted I stay at Nice Ugly."

It was thus they had christened a nondescript old house in Brooklyn Heights that they'd renovated and made comfortable, if not beautiful.

9

"Paula's there too," Sadd added.

I shook my head glumly. "She has got—and I'm keeping this *got*—*got* to go back to Boston. Poor Andy!"

"He was all for packing up the kids and coming too."

I groaned. "This is awful. And at Christmas, too! I hate whoever did this to us. It can't have been anybody at the party—they were all Sal's friends and mine. The bastard must have followed his victim down to the Village and into the store."

"*His* victim? Poisoners are more often women, I believe."

I shrugged. "The point is—my God, Sadd—who was the stuff meant for?"

He said nothing, and I thrashed impatiently, receiving a sharp warning from my ankle. "Ouch! Damn! Oh, why couldn't I have had the flu or something and missed Sal's opening? This is such a downer for her, and she's been so happy about the store and—and everything."

"*Everything* meaning what's-his-name?"

"Yes. Dwight Dunlop. Nice guy."

Sal, who had been a widow for as long as I, had met a pleasant widower her age at a small-business seminar at Cooper Union. They'd been married the week before.

"And I'll bet that in some crazy way"—I thrashed again—"she and Dwight are probably blaming themselves for this."

"Yes, they are." Sadd stood up. "They are also out in the hall champing to come in."

"Really?" Delighted, I reached for the bed jacket.

10

"Remind me to thank her for this. Where's the sleeve? There's everything on here but feathers."

"You're sure you're up to seeing them?" Sadd started toward the door.

"Of course I'm sure." I adjusted the lacy collar. "But I wish we had something to drink. They tell me in hospitals now you're allowed—"

"Have no fear." Sadd grinned. "Dwight's come well supplied—and with Dr. Cullen's permission as well."

And the next minute I was being smothered with hugs, heaped with flowers and candy, plied with champagne, and repeatedly asked if I could ever forgive them.

"Are you both insane?" I laughed and sipped happily. "Anybody would think you were responsible."

"Sal feels as if we are." Dwight Dunlop was a big, very personable man with a penchant for ribald jokes which he told extremely well. "If you hadn't come to our opening—"

"Rubbish." I kissed Sal as she hung over me, her kind, humorous face full of concern.

"Oh, Clara, this is too ghastly. Who could have done such a thing to you? I hope the police are working night and day."

"Police?" I looked at Sadd in alarm. He shook his head.

"No police." He refilled my glass. "You see, Clara believes that she was merely an accidental victim and the poison was intended for somebody else."

"Of course it was." I said. "I'm sorry for the poor thing who was supposed to get it—I hope it isn't any-

11

body we know, Sal—but it certainly wasn't me. Marvelous champagne."

They looked at each other—oddly, I thought—then Dwight shrugged and Sal said, "You haven't had one of your . . . er . . . cases lately that might involve somebody who . . . ?"

I laughed and sipped. *This* was the right medicine. "I haven't had a 'case,' as you put it, in over a year. My life has been bland and blameless. All I've done is play grandma and volunteer at the museum. By the way, thanks for the bed jacket. I feel like Jean Harlow."

"What?" Sal stared at me. "Oh—well, it's awfully frilly, but I had to grab it fast."

Dwight said, "Look what we brought you," and dumped a tote full of paperbacks on my bed.

"You angels!" I cried.

"And here's the fall issue of *The Armchair Detective*"—Sal reached into another bag—"and a first edition of L. P. Hartley's stories, and *The Rumpole Omnibus*."

"Sal!"

"I was going to save the Hartley for your birthday but—but nothing's too good for you now."

She bit her lip and gulped, and Dwight looked at her anxiously.

"Will you please quit that?" I said. "I'll be out of here in a couple of days and—"

"—and on a plane to Florida with me," said Sadd.

"Now you're talking!" Dwight was his jovial self again.

"Well, we'll see about Florida." I was feeling very

mellow. "I sort of hate to spend Christmas away from the kids. Now, how's business, and who's minding the store?"

Sal and Dwight both started to talk at once, and it was lovely and garbled and enthusiastic. There had been seventy—count 'em—seventy persons in already that day, sales had been brisk, and telephone orders above expectation. There was to be an article about them in some magazine and . . . I was conscious of growing tired. Sal sensed it at once.

"We're going." She stood up. "If I can get in again—"

"Don't you dare," I said. "You stay in that store and make money."

She leaned over and hugged me hard. "Take care of your dear, darling self."

I simply could not fathom this emotional parting. Dwight said, "Chin up!" and Sadd went out with them. I lay wondering what on earth . . .

Sadd came back and stood looking out the window. He said, "It's snowing. I haven't seen snow in five years."

I poured myself the last of the champagne and said, "Sadd, what's bugging everybody? Am I in worse shape than I've been told?"

"No, you're in good shape actually." He turned. "You're going to be fine."

"Then why is everybody acting like—"

"Acting *as if*. Clara, really, that is the most deplorable—"

"Oh, for God's sake, tell me what's wrong!" I pulled

off the bed jacket, which was tickling my chin unbearably. "Why is everybody acting *as if* I'm in mortal danger?"

"Because you are." He picked up my glass and drained it. "Whoever tried to kill you at that party . . . tried again last night."

3

I REMEMBER LOOKING SIDEWAYS AT THE RES-
idue of bubbles in the plastic champagne glass as Sadd
set it down on the bedside table.

I presume I said, "How?" because Sadd said, "Poison
again. Your supper tray."

A nurse came in with a pill in a paper cup. She
looked disapprovingly at the champagne bottle, then
said, "I guess we'll wait on the medication, Mrs.
Gamadge. Would you like something to eat?"

"No, thank you."

She went out, and I took a deep breath. Impossible.
Just plain impossible. Some mistake.

Sadd came back to the bed and picked up one of the
books. "A first edition of Hartley—what a treasure.
May I borrow the *Rumpole*? Er ... we're taking you
home. Tina and Paula will be here presently to help you
dress. Dr. Cullen is against it, but we don't want you to
spend another night on Bald Mountain."

"Sadd, listen to me—"

"No, you listen to *me*." He pulled up a plastic armchair and sat down leaning his elbows on the bed. "I'm

15

the designated breaker-of-the-bad-news. Your children can't bear to tell you. So 'listen up,' as the current expression goes—although why the addition of a mere preposition gives any more force—" He must have noticed my frozen face. "Clara, your accidental victim bit is out. Somebody has tried to kill you twice in one week, and we have to find out who and why. Who and why. That's what you'd say to anyone coming to you in a similar predicament."

He started to put the books back in the tote. "We decided not to bring in the police till we could talk it over with you. But Henry's hired a private detective who's sitting outside your door right now. His name is Dan Schenck, and it seems you knew his grandfather."

"Schenck!" Memories flooded back, almost drowning baleful thoughts. "Oh, the times that he and Henry Gamadge—"

"Nostalgia later, please. Right now, Clara, you must realize that either you help us or you're dead. Literally. And that would be a pity because your family would miss you and I'd lose a pied-à-terre in New York City."

"Sadd—"

"And by the way, Sal and Dwight and Dr. Cullen are the only persons other than us who know about the second poisoning attempt. So let me repeat Sal's question. Whose business have you been messing in lately that might result in somebody else turning killer?"

"And let me repeat my answer. Nobody's. That's my point." While Sadd was talking, I'd gone from bewilderment to terror to anger and was now back to bewilderment. "You heard what I said. It's over a year since anybody has asked me to 'mess' in their business."

"You're not involved in anything that's proving . . . unpropitious?"

"Not remotely." I swallowed rather hard. "Was it— was it arsenic again?"

"Yes."

"What was it in? Who found it?"

"Schenck found it." Sadd stood up. "It was in the sugar packet on the saucer of your coffee cup. He noticed a tear across the top and took it with him to be analyzed when he went off duty. His wife spells him—it seems they're in business together." He moved to the door, which I now realized was always kept closed. "Do you want to thank him? He probably saved your life."

"Of course I want to thank him. And talk to him about his grandfather. We won't tell him that I don't take sugar in my coffee. I take saccharin."

It was feeble, in poor taste, and I was instantly ashamed, but the whole business was incomprehensible. I didn't need this grotesque puzzle along with an aching ankle. The last year of my life had been singularly uneventful. I'd not had even one request for the kind of help or advice that my apprehensive family knows so often leads to trouble. It was all an insane dream. Surely I'd wake up presently in my brownstone on Sixty-third Street and regale my friends with an account of it.

A dark-haired young man with a mustache followed Sadd into the room.

"Dan Schenck!" I held out my arms, and he came

17

straight to the bed and kissed me. "You even *look* like your grandpa!"

"He thought the world of you, Mrs. Gamadge." His brown eyes were troubled. "I felt terrible when your son called me, but I'm glad it was me he called."

"So am I. Where do you live, Dan? Do you have a family?"

"Yep. My wife works with me, and we have a little boy. We live on West Fifty-ninth in an old building where the rents are frozen, thank God."

Sadd pulled up another chair. "It seems you're following in your grandfather's footsteps."

"Well, sort of. He was with the FBI. I'm in business for myself."

"So was he, practically, when he worked with Henry Gamadge." I smiled at the boy fondly. "I remember my husband saying, 'Schenck claims I'll get him fired yet.' During the war when there was gas rationing, Henry had the poor man chasing suspects because he had a government car. Once he sent him up to Connecticut, and your grandpa said, 'You'd better be able to tie this in to Bureau business,' and Henry said, 'I can—I'm certain it's murder.' "

Murder. The word hung there, and we stopped smiling. Dan said, "What can you give me to go on, Mrs. Gamadge?"

"Nothing," I said helplessly. "Not one thing." I explained how mundane the past year had been. Then I added, "You were an astute guy to notice. the sugar, Dan. I really owe you."

He sat forward. "Actually, it was one of those little

pink saccharin packets. I was standing near the rack when they brought the trays up—"

My eyes had locked with Sadd's, and Dan picked up on it at once.

"That's what you use?"

I nodded, and at that moment into the room walked Henry, Tina, Paula, and Dr. Cullen. Jolted though I felt, I managed, with Sadd's help, to make introductions. Then Dan said, "Back to my post," and went out.

It was the first time I'd seen Dr. Cullen except through a sort of haze. She was very tall, dark haired, dark eyed, and at the moment very businesslike. She said at once, "Mrs. Gamadge, I'm absolutely opposed to your going home." She took my hand and held it firmly. "I'm appalled at your situation, but it appears that you're well protected and I feel it's essential that you stay here a few more days and be monitored. At your age . . ."

She went on to rub it in about my age, and everybody stood looking glum. She ended by saying that she perfectly understood our terrible anxiety and concern, but if they or I insisted on my being removed, she would have to resign all responsibility.

I spoke up, trying to sound spunky and with it. "Dr. Cullen is absolutely right. I stay." I looked at my daughter. "And *you* darling, go at once back to your family."

Paula burst into tears and cast herself upon me sobbing that, yes, Henry was taking her to the airport at five but how could she bear to leave when . . . et cetera, et cetera. I patted and consoled her, promised I would come to Boston right after Christmas, and Tina took her into the bathroom to mop up. No one else had moved, and Dr. Cullen, whom I'd have expected to flee during such a pitiful outburst, had stood motionless and grave throughout. Now she said quietly, "You all have my total sympathy. I'll be honest—this experience is a first for me. I've had some unusual cases, but I've never encountered—er—"

"—a nice elderly lady with a contract out on her," said Sadd.

I giggled weakly, and Henry looked as if he was trying not to. The nurse came back in with my pill, and Dr. Cullen said, "This tranquilizer should help." I gulped the huge thing, and she went on, moving toward the door, "We've thought it best not to discuss this matter with the floor staff. Sister Agnes has been told that the surveillance is required to protect you from an undisclosed threat—"

"I love euphemisms," murmured Sadd.

"—and she understands that your meals will be brought up from the cafeteria by your family or the person guarding you." Dr. Cullen suddenly stopped, briskness gone, and came back to my bed. "I wish there were something I could do."

I held out my hand. "You've done it, Doctor, and we thank you. May I call you in the middle of the night if need be?"

She reached for a pad on my bedside table and scribbled. "Here's my number at home. Call it whenever you please."

"You're a peach."

She went out, and Henry opened a brown paper bag. He said, "Let's have some wine and then a conference."

A corkscrew was produced, Tina and Paula emerged from the bathroom, and I asked them to collect the plastic glasses and rinse them.

"You've been tippling already?" said Tina.

"Yes. Sal and Dwight were here with champagne."

"How's the store going?" asked Henry.

"Super, I'm glad to say."

"Clara's just had a pill, so she'll pass." Sadd accepted a glass from Tina.

"Like fun I will."

"Mom!" Paula had always been my vigilant child.

"And give some to Dan," I said.

"He's on duty." Henry looked severe. "Do you want him disbarred or unfrocked or stripped of his buttons or branded or flogged—"

"And that reminds me, dear, you are not to spend your own money on Dan. I'll take care of him. Actually, guard duty is not what a private investigator does. After all, he's a detective—"

"He offered to do this, Mom." Henry looked around, wine bottle poised. "He said his grandparents used to talk about the favors you and Dad did them. And don't worry"—Henry corked the bottle, looking grim—"he'll get a chance to detect. Everybody set? Then I have the floor."

They settled into chairs, Paula beside the bed clinging to my hand. In the darkness outside the window great flakes descended whitely. Henry leaned back in the plastic armchair and stretched out his legs in a manner achingly like his father. Gazing at me, he said, "Somebody who knew you were at the party for Pushing Murder and who also knows you take saccharin in your coffee wants you dead." He cleared his throat. "Let's tackle the party first: who was there that you knew?"

"I knew practically everybody." It was an unsatisfactory answer but the truth. "They were all Sal's friends and mine. Most of us had been in and out of the store all week helping her." I thought for an instant, then added, feeling injured, "You'd think some of them would have been in to see me. They must all know what happened."

"They've been flooding in here," said Tina.

"What?"

Henry said, "First you were in too much shock to see them, then after the second poisoning attempt we didn't dare let anybody up."

"Henry! They're my friends!"

"One of them may not be."

There was a brief silence, then I grumbled, "You let Sal and Dwight up."

Henry shrugged. "They're like us—above suspicion."

We were silent again. Sadd took a book from his pocket and put it back again. Tina looked at her watch and then at Paula, who shook her head and clung tighter to my hand. Looking at the runny window, I said gently, "Leave plenty of time. La Guardia will be a zoo."

"We'll make it." Henry sat forward. "Now, Mother!"

When my son, to whom I'm always "Mom," says "Mother" in that tone, I know I'm on the carpet.

Feeling guilty for absolutely no reason I could think of, I said, "Yes, dear?"

"Has anyone approached you lately for help?"

Fourth time, wearily, "No."

"You haven't even had a conversation that has touched on a, shall we say, sensitive area?"

"Not even a conversation."

"You're certain? Think hard."

"I've thought. For the past year my life has been boringly undisturbed."

"No one has—even indirectly—uttered a cry for help?"

"No cry for help."

"Then," said Henry, "I can only think of one thing." He leaned back in his chair and looked at the ceiling. "Someone is about to. And someone else knows it and doesn't like it."

And the next day the cry came.

4

IT CAME IN THE FORM OF A PHONE CALL TO
my home, where Sadd had gone at my request to collect
mail and sundries.

I'd spent a miserably restless night, having declined a
sleeping pill because I wanted to think, then found that
all I could think about was whether I'd get out of this
place alive. "The readiness is all," I quoted to myself
but wondered if Hamlet would have been that cool if
he'd found himself in my situation; at least *he* could
walk around while he philosophized.

I lay listening to the doleful sounds of a hospital at
night. Calls and cries, sobs and snores, nurses' feet
responding ... St. Victor's was a very old hospital for-
merly staffed, I'd been told, entirely by nuns, now more
by lay persons. I'd passed and repassed it often in the
last few weeks on my way down to help Sal and
Dwight. I'd always loved this part of New York. I'd
bought my wedding dress at Wanamaker because Aunt
Robbie, the beloved woman who raised me, said my
mother, whom I never knew, had bought hers there.

24

Greenwich Village, familiar and fascinating. Who had spoiled it for me and why?

I wiped dampness from my eyes and moved my foot gingerly. Not bad. It hardly hurt at all. A nice young orthopedist had been in to ask me how I was doing and say I might even take a spin down the hall in a wheelchair tomorrow. What did the hall look like? Equipment on wheels, busyness, possibly a small commotion, a face known (or unknown) to me—and even with Dan at my side—

I sat up in bed and snapped on the reading light. Kit Schenck, Dan's wife, had been seated outside my door since eleven o'clock. I'd asked her to leave it open, hating the enclosed feeling. I half called, half whispered, "What time is it, Kit?"

"Two-thirty."

"Come in and talk."

"Okay."

Kit was a wiry young woman with short, curly hair and a wide smile. She wore the ubiquitous jeans and a black sweater. She put a chair between my bed and the door, and we chatted. I discovered that her name had been Gail Kitenski, that her son and my grandson were both in the fifth grade and both having trouble with arithmetic. Then Kit wanted to talk about my "case," but I said this was no hour to discuss anything but pleasant, solvable problems like what ten-year-olds might want for Christmas. I suppose I fell asleep because the next thing I knew the room was bright with sun and Kit was walking through the door with a tray. She said, "I hope you like French toast."

"I love it."

"Dan will be in shortly. I'm here till he comes. Sorry, but I think the door should be shut. See you tonight."

Kit left, and I poured syrup, my spirits brightening with the morning. The door was pushed open, and Sadd backed in carrying a tote and a cup of coffee. He was wearing an old red parka of my husband's.

"Good." I looked fondly at the thing. "You found it."

"And thank heaven. The snow has stopped, but it's absolutely freezing."

"Sadd, I know how you hate the cold. You're a saint to be here."

"Am I not?" He hoisted the tote onto the bed. "I hope I've remembered everything. You got a phone call while I was at your place."

I froze, fork in midair, remembering my son's words. Sadd put his coffee down and shrugged off the parka. "Who is Janet Folsom?"

Relieved, I completed the bite. "Oh, dear Jan. Not even remotely sinister. She used to be a nun."

"Why would that preclude her being sinister?"

"Look at these Christmas cards!" I dug into the tote. "And I haven't even finished writing mine yet."

"I'd say your priorities were elsewhere this year." He sipped his coffee. "Don't you want to know what your nonsinister friend Janet had to say?"

"Of course." I dug deeper. "Address book, cards, stamps, hairbrush, bathrobe, slippers. You dear thing, I believe you've remembered everything."

"She said she was upset and frightened about something and needed your help."

26

I sat back—jerked, actually—against my pillow. Dan put his head in the door.

"Reporting for duty."

Sadd said, "Come in, Dan. You'll want to hear this." Dan was in like a flash. Sadd took a banana from my tray. "May I have half of this?"

I nodded, and he sat down, peeling it. "I went to Mrs. Gamadge's home on Sixty-third Street this morning to fetch some things for her. I was just getting out of the elevator—it opens directly into her living room—when the phone rang." Sadd took a bite of banana. "It was rather eerie—that sudden ring in the empty room."

"Who was it?" asked Dan.

I said, "An old friend of mine named Janet Folsom." I looked at my fork. "She's a widow. She's frightened about something and wants my help."

Dan pulled up a chair and sat on the edge of it. "Did she know—or did she say she knew—that Mrs. Gamadge was in the hospital?"

"No." Sadd ate more of the banana. "I told her, and she seemed distressed. She wanted to know why, and I said you'd had an accident but didn't elaborate. She asked if she could come see you."

"No," said Dan.

"But, Dan, Janet is an old and dear—"

"At least not till I see her first. Where does she live?"

"Fairfield, Connecticut."

"But at the moment," said Sadd, "she's in Room 312 at the Plaza."

"The Plaza," I said dreamily. The name still conjured up memories of its dear, old elegance. I'd spent my wedding night at the Plaza in July of 1941 and vividly recall catching a glimpse of the bill and gasping at my bridegroom's extravagance. "Mr. and Mrs. Henry Gamadge, Tenth Floor Suite, $22.50."

Dan stood up. "I'll go see Mrs. Folsom tonight. Did you tell her what hospital, Mr. Saddlier?"

"I'm afraid I did." Sadd looked remorseful. "She asked, and before I could stop to think—"

"Not a problem." Dan reached for the phone. "I'll call her. But two to one she's on her way down here now."

How right he was. There was no answer in Room 312 at the Plaza, and Dan had scarcely hung up when the phone rang. A second instrument had been put in the room, and Dan or Kit listened to calls. I'd chatted with solicitous friends, but "No Visitors" was still enforced.

Dan picked up his receiver, and I picked up mine.

"Clara! It's Jan Folsom—my God, are you all right?"

"Well, yes and no, Jan. My cousin told me you called the apartment. How are you?"

"How am *I*? How are *you*? He wouldn't tell me a thing. Did you fall or something? I'm down at the desk, and they won't let me up. Please tell them to! I promise not to talk about my trouble—that can wait. I'd just like to see you!"

I looked piteously at Dan. He nodded and pointed to Sadd.

"All right, Jan. My cousin is here now, and he'll come down for you. His name is Charles Saddlier."

"Yes, he told me. I think I knew his wife. Was she Harriet Ames?"

"Sure was." I hung up. "She knew Harriet, Sadd."

"Almost as reassuring as having been a nun." He stood up. "I've eaten your whole banana. Do you want another?"

"No." My appetite had sharply diminished. "Will you take the tray, please?"

Dan picked it up and followed Sadd to the door. He said, "I'll wait for them at the elevator. I want a word with the lady first."

I lay back trying to remember everything I knew about Janet Folsom.

She'd been beautiful, still was. How old was Janet? Some years younger than I, maybe sixty. Her mother had been a friend of Aunt Robbie's. Janet was an intriguing combination of great beauty and deep religious faith. In her early twenties she had entered a Benedictine convent but, never strong, had suffered a breakdown and had been reluctantly and lovingly released by that order. Almost at once, a shy young millionaire, Lewis Folsom, who had hoped to marry her, reappeared on the scene, and Janet was swept through what Evelyn Waugh once called "the hundred and one horrors of a fashionable wedding." Within a year the robust Lewis died of hepatitis, and the delicate Janet survived to perform endless good works and support innumerable good causes. For a few years she'd been a member of my bridge club along with Sal. But Janet's life became more and more devoted to her charities, and we saw less and less of her.

I'd last seen Janet about a year ago at a banquet in her honor given by St. Francis Seminary in Fairfield, marking the thirtieth anniversary of the Lewis Folsom scholarship fund. She had looked stunning in an azure blue silk gown created for her by some giant of the designing world, and Sal, sitting beside me, had remarked glumly that Janet's figure was as good as ever. Her ash-blond hair, expertly maintained ash-blond, brushed the great diamonds in her ears, her fingers glittered with the same, and around her neck was a little square of brown burlap on a string. It was, a priest at our table told us, the scapular of the Order of St. Benedict, which she never removed.

Who on earth would want to frighten or upset Janet Folsom?

I heard the elevator door open, then voices—Janet's and Dan's—and Sadd appeared at my door looking over his shoulder. Janet's voice grew agitated.

"What's up?" I said.

Sadd gave a puzzled shrug and stood looking toward them. The usual traffic of nurses and berobed patients passed, some looking curiously back toward what was now the sobbing sound of Janet's voice.

This was intolerable. "Dammit, Sadd, tell Dan to let her in!"

But Janet let herself in. She streaked past Sadd weeping and gasping, "My fault! All my fault! I did it, Clara, I nearly got you killed!" And now I was in her throttling embrace, damp from the snow still clinging to her coat. "And look—I've soaked you! Nice work, Janet—give her pneumonia, too!" She dropped the coat, a lovely cashmere one, to the floor. "Oh, Clara, what have I done? Are you still horribly sick? And let me see your poor ankle!"

She was tugging at my covers. I slapped her hand, then kissed it.

"Let me alone, idiot, and sit down. I don't know what you've done, but we're all very interested in finding out."

Dan had closed the door quickly, and now he and Sadd stood at the foot of the bed in that confused state of embarrassment and distress that men exhibit when women make scenes. Janet sank into the chair Dan had pushed to the bed, her face in her hands.

The door opened, and Dr. Cullen walked in with Sister Agnes. I felt a wild desire to laugh. Were introductions in order? How about, "Dr. Cullen, Sister, this is a dear friend who says she's responsible for the attacks on my life"? The nice doctor saved me by merely saying, "You have visitors—we won't stay. How do you feel?"

"Much better."

She left, nodding with a smile to the visitors she'd met, and politely ignoring the bowed figure of the one she had not. Sister did the same but could not resist a compassionate glance at poor Janet.

As the door shut Dan said, "Mrs. Folsom, please tell us what this is all about."

Janet wiped her eyes, straightened in the chair, and said, "The whole ghastly business began—"

She broke off, eyes wide, staring at the scattered Christmas cards on my bed.

"My God—is that your mail?" She stood up, pawing through it. "Is there more?" She upended the tote, and

31

its contents went flying. We watched her, transfixed. "Not here. Not here yet. Or else he's got it. When did all this come?"

Sadd said, "I picked it up from Clara's box this morning."

"Then it's a wonder you're still alive." She stared at him. "Or is this yesterday's mail?"

"It's everything since Sunday. Today's hasn't been delivered yet." Sadd sounded amazingly sane, considering Janet's exhibition.

The door opened again, and Henry walked in, pulling off his scarf. "Tina's holding down the office." He took in our tense tableau. "Am I de trop?"

"Not at all, dear." Was *I* managing to sound sane? "Janet, this is my son, Henry. Henry, this is a friend of mine, Janet Folsom, who says she did it and is here to confess all."

"Don't joke, Clara." She shook hands with Henry nervously. "I did do it—or as good as did it." She began to weep again.

Dan was picking up the scattered objects from the tote, and Sadd rescued the coat and hung it in the closet. I hauled myself up straighter in bed and said, "Dan, lock that door."

"You can't lock hospital doors, Mrs. Gamadge."

"Then put a chair against it, and sit on it, and somebody sit on Dan. Nobody's getting in here till we have Janet's story."

Henry picked up the phone. "No calls to Room 220. Mrs. Gamadge needs rest. This is her son. I'll stop for messages later."

They dispersed about the room. Sadd in the plastic armchair, Henry beside him, Dan leaning on the windowsill, snow starting up again behind him. Janet remained by my bed, her eyes fixed on my face. Then, something, not a premonition—I don't have them—but something made me say, "I don't want the police in on this. Promise me, Henry."

The three men said, "Why?"

Now I knew what that "something" was; it had been dawning on me fuzzily ever since Janet burst in. Someone whom she and I knew was trying to kill me, and I was about to learn who it was. Did I know this someone's family? parents? husband? wife? Quite possibly. The thought of the shock and grief in store for them oppressed me. I must try to spare them what I could. The police couldn't and wouldn't.

Janet's eyes had not left mine. I was sure she knew my thoughts. She said, "Don't promise her, Henry."

He said, "Start talking, Mrs. Folsom."

Janet cleared her throat. She spoke calmly now, looking down at her clasped hands. "About thirty years ago—1965 to be precise—I opened a home for children of Cuban refugees. It was the year Castro allowed them to leave and they poured over. The homelessness and hardships were awful. I wanted to model my home on Pearl Buck's Welcome House, the place she started in the forties for Asian children. My husband and I—he's been dead many years—always admired Mrs. Buck. I bought a big old farmhouse in a town called Bryantville in central Connecticut and staffed it mostly with people from the town. They were all wonderful. Except one."

Her eyes went to the blurry white window behind Dan. None of us moved. Perhaps trying to delay the revelation, I said, "I remember the place. Didn't you call it St. Elizabeth's Home?"

"Yes. For Mother Elizabeth Seton. She had children. Well, it went marvelously for about three years. From the start, donations poured in, and we began to accumulate more money than we needed. That can be worse than not having enough. Often when places of this kind get too affluent, they're wide open for all kinds of scams and hanky-panky."

Sadd said, "Boys Town, for one."

"Yes—remember that scandal? But they recouped honorably. You can only respect that. Of course, we were a much smaller operation, and most of the money was mine. Even so, when the blow fell . . ." Janet took a tissue from her pocketbook and blew her nose. Her eyes came back to mine.

"The director of St. Elizabeth's, whom I'd chosen myself, was a man named Allen Quinn. He came with glowing letters of recommendation from some bishop in New Mexico, but I must confess"—now her look went askew—"that it was his personality that sold me. He was a good-looking man in his forties, and he radiated charm and capability. The staff adored him, the kids adored him, and I adored him, right up to the minute that he disappeared with all the money."

Janet stopped talking, and there was utter silence. Then Sadd said briskly, "How about elevenses?"

"Good idea." Henry stood up. "Where's your sherry,

34

Mom?" I pointed to the bedside cabinet. "Did you ever catch the charming rascal, Mrs. Folsom?"

"No."

Dan said, "But you tried to and in the process found out that his references had all been faked."

"Everything about him was fake"—Janet smiled wanly—"including his name. The references were on letterhead stolen from the bishop's office during a fund-raising campaign for the diocese—I don't have to tell you what happened to the funds. The bishop told me his investigation revealed that this man had been in prison under the name Howard de Lamier, and that he'd run through a number of other philanthropies, always managing to evaporate."

There was an imperious knock on the door, and Dan admitted the nurse with my pill. This time it was the sherry bottle in Henry's hand that caught her disapproving eye, and she stopped dead.

"I haven't had any yet," I said hastily.

She poured water from my jug, handed me the enormous pellet—why are they always the size of something you'd give a horse?—and watched me down it. Then she went out, her walk suggesting that she was rolling her eyes to heaven.

Janet spoke now without moving a muscle. "Of course we tried to trace him, and of course we had no luck. My donors were wonderful. Some of them suggested that we launch a drive to start again, but how could they know the amount of capital it had taken? It wouldn't have been fair to my other charities. St. Elizabeth's closed less than a year later. Fortunately, I was kept busy during that time finding homes for the children, and I almost forgot Allen Quinn, alias Howard de Lamier, alias God-knows-who. I hadn't thought of him in years till last week when I saw him at his wedding. You were there too, Clara."

My heart gave a great lurch.

"He was marrying Sal. His new name is Dwight Dunlop."

5

DAN JERKED AWAY FROM THE WINDOW, AND it was the only motion in the room. A dazed question was forming in my head, but I couldn't speak; I could only recall Dwight Dunlop's jovial presence beside my bed yesterday. Sadd and Henry simply stared at Janet, and she appeared unable to look at any of us. Her flamboyant outrage was gone, her composure was gone, and she sat with closed eyes, tears streaming from beneath the lids.

I somehow got out my question. "Janet . . . if you've threatened to expose him—I assume you have—why isn't it *you* he wants to kill?"

"Oh, wouldn't he love to!" Her eyes flew open. "Unfortunately for him, I was in Denver all last week at a UNICEF meeting." She gulped. "And like a fool, I'd gone and involved you."

"How?"

Dan said, "You wrote to Mrs. Gamadge about him, and he knows it."

She nodded wretchedly. "I did everything wrong. I was desperate to protect Sal. Oh, I've botched it so badly!"

"Janet"—I took hold of her wrist, my curiosity getting the better of my dismay—"describe the awful moment when you recognized him."

She loosened my fingers, got up, and began to move about the room tugging at the neck of her exquisite silk blouse. The string of the scapular came into sight, and she thrust it back with shaking fingers. She said, "I was late for that wedding. I don't know if you remember."

"Yes, I do. The house was jammed." I looked at the others. "Sal's son and his wife gave it. They have a nice big house in New Jersey, and there must have been fifty or sixty—"

"Clara," said Sadd, "you sound like a society columnist covering an earthquake."

"Sorry. Go on, Jan."

"I spotted you when I came in so I went over to say hello."

"I remember. I remember."

"Sal and—and that man were in front of the fireplace with some people around them. First I saw her, and you said, 'Doesn't Sal look happy?' And then I saw him. I turned around quickly and told you I needed the bathroom."

"I remember. I remember. You said you'd be right back, and you never came."

"God, no." Janet's hand went to her throat again. She came back to her chair. "I prayed he hadn't seen me. I thought he hadn't. But the next night the phone rang. He was calling from some restaurant where he and Sal were having dinner."

38

There was a tap on the door, and a nurse I'd never seen before looked in. "Lunchtime. I understand your meals are brought up from the cafeteria. Who is—"

"Jeeze, I'm a fine one!" Dan slapped his head. "What'll it be, Mrs. Gamadge?"

"Forget it. I couldn't eat a bite."

"Now what have I done?" wailed Janet as the nurse withdrew. "You need to keep your strength up, and I've completely wiped out your appetite."

"Go on, Mrs. Folsom," said my unfeeling son. "He called you from the restaurant."

"Yes, and you never heard a more pitiful and pleading account of his 'reform.' He was through with scams, he was on the straight and narrow. Did I want to destroy Sal's happiness and his? Surely I would not expose him when he'd finally found true love and peace of mind."

"Little Gloria, happy at last," murmured Sadd.

"But you weren't buying," said Dan.

"You bet I wasn't." Janet stood up again, hesitated, then walked to the closet and took out her coat. "I told him—making the biggest mistake of my life—that I'd give him twenty-four hours to get out of Sal's life. He asked me if I knew what it would do to her morale if he went, and I said I knew what it would do to her bank account if he stayed. More protestations of a new leaf, et cetera, but I knew he was about as reformable as Beelzebub—and wasn't I just proved right!" Angrily, she pulled on her coat.

Henry said, "It didn't occur to you to fake belief in him till you could go to the police?"

"With what?" Janet sat down again clutching her coat. "I had the stuff from St. Elizabeth's, but that was thirty years ago. Even if I could have dug up something recent, all I could think of was the inquiries and the litigation and Sal's prolonged horror and humiliation, and I just decided to get rid of him quick. So I said, 'You heard me—twenty-four hours,' and he said could he have till Sunday, the day the store opened, because it would break Sal's heart if he went before that." Her voice shook. "My own heart was just about breaking, so I said, 'Okay, Sunday,' and then I blew it."

Sadd said, "You told him you were writing to Clara."

"Yes." She looked at me tragically. "I said, 'But all this is going in a letter to Clara Gamadge—you've met her—and she and I will go to Sal together. The letter will be mailed Sunday, the day of the party, and she'll have it by Tuesday so you'd better be gone.' "

Tuesday. Today. All three men checked watches. Dan looked at me. "Noon. What time does your mail come?"

"Around two," I said. "Janet, did he ask you not to speak to me before the letter arrived?"

"He didn't ask, he *told* me not to—or I'd be sorry. But I panicked and had to call you and tell you what I'd done—and oh, God, it's so much worse than what I *thought* I'd done!"

She began to tremble violently, huddling in the chair. In a flash, Dan was at my side, his hand outstretched. "The key to your mailbox."

"Mr. Saddlier has it."

Dan swung his hand toward Sadd, who dug in his pocket. Janet was off the chair. "I'm going with you."

"No way, Mrs. Folsom." Dan was definite. "You're still in Denver if you want to keep living. Get in a cab and go straight back to the Plaza. Don't open your door to anybody till I can get protection for you. If I didn't know Dunlop had other business today, I wouldn't let you go alone."

I said nervously, "I don't suppose not having a key to the mailbox will faze him."

"Piece of cake." Dan was at the door. "He's probably on your street right now waiting for the delivery."

"Good luck to him in this weather." Sadd shuddered, and I said hastily, "All my keys are on that ring, Dan. Wait in the vestibule. I don't care if he freezes, but you don't have to."

He looked back at us. "Who'll fill in for me here?"

I said, "No one needs to. We know where he is." The thought made me a little sick.

Dan shook his head. "We won't know where he is after two o'clock, and suppose I'm delayed getting back here?"

"I'd planned to stay the afternoon anyway." Sadd pulled a book from his pocket, and Dan left.

Janet looked at Henry wanly. "Can you ever forgive me?"

"Look—you've fingered him for us. At least we know who has it in for Mom. Can I get you a cab?"

"No, thank you. I want to visit the chapel here first."

"Chapel?" I said, surprised.

"Oh, yes. It's a lovely little one. In the children's

wing. It even has a tiny library. I used to visit it often."
She buttoned her coat and added simply, "My husband
died in this hospital, you know."

"Really, Janet?" Surprise jerked me out of my terrible
concern for her.

"Yes, we used to have an apartment on Ninth Street
for coming into New York to the theater. Lewis loved
the theater. He was taken ill the night we'd been to see
Julie Andrews in *The Boy Friend*—why does one remember details like that?—and he was brought here. He
never left the hospital." She came to the bed and kissed
me. "Will you call me at the Plaza as soon as that
young man—Dan, is it?—gets back with the letter,
please God?" She held out her hand to Sadd as he stood
up. "They call you Sadd, as I recall. I knew Harriet."

"So Clara said. Shall I come down with you?"

"Absolutely not."

Henry had been fidgeting as his father always did
when his mind was teeming. Janet held out her hand to
him, and he said, "Mrs. Folsom—"

"Janet."

"Janet—for God's sake, be careful. No way is this
man going to give up his wife and his meal ticket."

She continued to hold his hand, nodding almost re-
flectively. Then she said, "If we can get that letter from
your mother's mailbox, she's in the clear. Right?"

"I guess so, but you'll still—"

"Henry, I'll be so happy to free Clara from this night-
mare, I don't think anything would frighten me." She
took a pair of gloves from her coat pocket. "Did any of
you ever see the play *Murder in the Cathedral*?"

42

"I did," said Sadd. "And I've read it a dozen times."

Janet took a step toward him eagerly. "Do you remember what Thomas à Becket says to his friends when they tell him his murderers are at the door?"

Sadd blinked at the ceiling. "Something to the effect . . . that . . . they shouldn't worry because . . ." He shook his head. "Finish it for me."

" 'I am in no danger; only near to death.' " Janet smiled at us serenely and went out.

"That," said Sadd sitting down again, "is what I call spiritual poise."

"And this whole business," I said, lying back exhausted, "is what *I* call rotten and shocking. My poor, poor Sal!"

"Tina's going to be horrified." Henry wrapped his scarf about his neck. "She's fond of Sal."

"Aren't we all?" Sadd stared out the streaked window. "It's ghastly. Ghastly."

Ghastly. Henry came to the bed to kiss me, and I fingered the stubby fringe of his scarf. "Do me a favor?"

"Of course."

"I'm going to call Sal. I want to know if she has even a remote inkling. Will you listen in?"

"Sure."

I checked the pad where Sal had scribbled the number for Pushing Murder, punched numbers, and got a voice that said, "Jiffy Cleaners." Damn. I started again, realized my hand was shaking, and looked imploringly at Henry. He said, "I'll do it." Sadd stood up and handed me the other receiver.

"Let Henry talk. You listen."

Sal's cheery voice said, "Pushing Murder."

"Sal—it's Henry Gamadge."

"Hi, Henry. How's your mom?"

"Pretty good."

"I tried to get her a while ago, but they said no calls."

"She just needs rest. How's business?"

"Kind of slow. I wish it would stop snowing."

"Is Dwight there?"

"No, he's gone out to do errands."

Oh, God.

"When do you expect him back?"

"I have no idea. Shall I have him call you?"

"No, it's not important."

"Are you calling from the hospital? Can I speak to Clara?"

"Er—I'm at the office."

"Oh. Well, come see us soon."

"I'll do that. Bye, Sal."

He hung up, and I let my receiver drop beside me. Sadd said, "Unconscious of the sword of Damocles?"

"Totally."

Henry stood staring at the phone. He said, "As I see it, there are three possible scenarios. One—"

The door was pushed open, and Sister Agnes backed in with a tray. She said, "I thought a cup of tea might . . ." Sister's instructions had evidently included a suggestion to pamper this slightly cuckoo old lady. "And some macaroons. I made them myself."

"Sister, you're a saint." Sadd helped himself to one of the macaroons and Henry to another. I grabbed the last one as she smiled and withdrew. "Go on, Henry. One?"

"One, Dunlop gets the letter, Clara is safe, and Janet is dead. Two, Dan gets the letter, and Clara's back in jeopardy. Three, he doesn't return from his 'errands.' He's vamoosed, and Sal never sees him again."

"Not the last. Not that man." I lay back feeling horribly depressed.

Sadd said, "This is what I don't understand: other than his meal ticket, what good is Sal to him? Small specialty stores—in particular bookstores—are notoriously shaky propositions. They seldom make a dime. Unless Sal has a lot of money—"

"She does," I said wearily.

"What?" The two spoke as one.

"Well, quite a bit. Her brother died last year and left her some. That's what she's using."

Henry rewrapped his scarf. "Then Dunlop will have to move fast—before she runs through it all."

6

FOUR O'CLOCK. WHERE WAS DAN?

Sister had been back to take my blood pressure. She'd clucked approvingly at my progress, admired the nightgown Tina had sent me, and we'd talked about the snow. I suppose I dozed. The early kind of winter darkness was descending on the room, and Sadd, my protector, was asleep in his chair. The same tinny sound of a carol drifted up from the street. This time it was "Joy to the World."

The hall was unusually quiet, or was my imagination creating a sinister lull during which a visitor might pad to my door? Kit was due on duty in an hour. Oh, Dan, where are you? Please, God, don't let me have to tell his wife—

The phone rang. Sadd woke up with a start as I grabbed my receiver.

"Hi, Clara, this is Dwight."

No. No. *No!*

"Sal said Henry called me. Is he there?"

"No." This one aloud.

"She said you couldn't take calls this morning. Not a setback, I hope."

"No." Did I know another word? Sadd, thank God, had picked up the other receiver.

"Dwight, this is Sadd. Clara's been told the facts, and she's pretty shocked, naturally."

"Of course she is, poor dear. Are you still on, Clara?"

"Yes." Ah—a new word.

"You mustn't worry, my dear. We'll get to the bottom of this awful business. Make them give you a good strong sleeping pill and go off remembering we're all rooting for you."

I managed to add "Thank you" to my vocabulary and hung up. Sadd did the same, looking rather shaken. He said, "My God, the man has nerves of steel. Does he think he's in the clear? Does this mean he has the letter? What happened while I was asleep at my post?"

"Nothing. Oh, where's Dan?"

Sadd looked around dazedly. "Not back yet? What time is it?"

"After four."

He ran his hands through his hair. "Let me relieve myself before I have to contemplate another crisis."

He went into the bathroom, and I lay back in a stew. That voice on the phone with its fake concern had reduced me to jelly. I was desperate for outside contact, for information and reassurance—even consolation. I would *not* call Henry and Tina; they'd been subjected to enough. I only hoped Paula would not call *me*; the slightest indication of my distraught state, and she'd be on a plane back to New York.

47

Oh, Dan, *come*.

It was Kit who came. Usually she put her head in the door and said, "Reporting for duty." This time she walked into the room and up to the bed and said, "Now, don't be upset."

Had the girl never studied psychology? That command, of all commands, sends one into a distractedly upset state. I grabbed her arm.

"What? What?"

"Dan was mugged in the hospital garage. He's okay."

"What's 'okay'? What's 'okay'?" I had a case of the repeats.

"He has abrasions and a broken wrist. It's being set down in Emergency."

I flung back my covers. "Get me a wheelchair!"

"Mrs. Gamadge—no!"

"Clara, are you mad?" Sadd emerged from the bathroom to see my cast flailing.

I said, "Dan's been hurt, and I'm going—"

"Not badly," protested Kit, "and he's coming up here just as soon as—"

"Either I get a wheelchair, or I *crawl* down to Emergency."

"Hold on a second." Kit took both my hands. "You told me last night that the orthopedist said maybe you could have a wheelchair today."

"He did! He did!" The repeats were back like hiccups.

"Let me check and see if he left word. If he did, you get one."

48

She started for the door, and Sadd said, "I don't think I've met this young lady. Dan's wife, right?"

"Kit, this is my cousin, Mr. Saddlier." Quick and ungracious. "Get the chair." Kit smiled at Sadd and left.

"Attractive," said Sadd, and I muttered something to the effect that he'd notice attractiveness in a woman who was pushing him off a cliff. I added, "Hand me my bathrobe, please. It's in the closet."

"Not till we know if you need it, Clara. Get back under the covers. I suppose you know you're still a target till we find out what happened to Dan."

"I just know one thing: Dan's grandparents were friends of mine, and if anything serious—"

"Clara, he's a detective for heaven's sake. You know this is all in a day's work."

"I don't care. He has a nice wife and a little boy Hen's age."

"You sound mawkish and unprofessional."

Kit came through the door followed by Disapproving Nurse pushing a wheelchair. Kit said, "Look what I found! Where's your robe?"

They helped me into it, and with D.N. on one side and Kit on the other, I emerged gingerly from the bed. D.N. said, "Put your weight on the good leg," and I revolved and sank triumphantly into place.

"Onward and upward," said Sadd.

"Downward, actually," I said, "to Emergency."

"Emergency?" D.N. looked aghast.

Why had I opened my mouth? "Well, a friend of mine is being treated there. I hoped I could—"

49

"Mrs. Gamadge, I'm sure the doctor only meant for you to take a turn up and down the hall."

"Perfectly right. Up and down the hall," I said. She patted my shoulder and departed. "But she didn't say *which* hall," I added, and Kit began to laugh. Sadd said, "Jesuitical reasoning if ever I heard it."

"Is there an elevator somewhere out of sight?" I asked.

"Right around the corner," said Kit. She asked Sadd to push because she wanted her hands free.

It was an odd feeling of emergence into the world again. My room had been a cocoon for what seemed ages, and the hall felt like another country. I gazed from left to right into rooms where poor, recumbent souls gazed back. We passed people pushing intravenous apparatus on casters and people hobbling on crutches; we stopped for a bed rolling out of a room bearing a white-faced, wide-eyed girl. I thought grimly that at least none of them had to fear an unguarded door, a threatening presence. Kit walked beside me, her vigilant, sweeping glance taking in everything.

We turned at the end of the hall where a little corner waiting room boasted a Christmas tree. Two other occupants of wheelchairs and their visitors looked at us as we stopped before the elevator.

Kit said, "We don't get in here with anybody else. If somebody makes a run for it as the door starts to close, we get out."

No one did, and down we went. The door opened, and we emerged to confront Dan, a badly ripped parka over his shoulders, his right arm in a cast from palm to elbow, and evidence of a struggle on his face and in his hair.

He looked astonished, then aghast. "Turn right around and get back in that elevator!"

"No, siree." I grabbed his good hand. "I'm out of my cage, and I love it. Where can we go for a drink?"

Dan laughed. "There's a waiting room at the end of this hall. However, much as I could use a drink—"

"There's a packie across the street," said Sadd. "I'm getting to know this neighborhood."

"What's a packie?" asked Kit, her eyes on the stream of passersby.

Sadd sighed. "What children. Aren't liquor stores called that anymore?"

"Look!" Over the flow of moving heads I saw a sign with an arrow: TO CHAPEL. I pointed to it. "There lies salvation."

Sadd looked startled. "Drinks in the chapel?"

"Of course not. In the library next to it that Janet told us about."

"I'll make it wine," said Sadd. "That will be more appropriate for chapel precincts." He took off.

Dan and Kit, who had not for a minute relaxed their vigilance, began to laugh. Dan said, "I wish Gramps and Mr. Gamadge were here."

"Maybe they are, Dan." I felt suddenly somber. "When we get to the chapel, we'll invoke their spirits. Now, start talking."

"When we get there. Honey, will you do the chair?"

We rolled on in silence. I decided to hear Dan's story before I told him about Dwight's call. I ground my teeth at the thought of the man. Had he snagged the letter? I had a sinking feeling that Dan would have laid it in my lap at once if he had it.

We turned a corner, and another sign—CHILDREN'S WING—appeared over a door to a glass-enclosed passage. We went down the passage, and I looked out with wonder at the dense, snow-slowed traffic and the sagging ropes of Christmas lights. Strangely, the world outside one's own has a way of going on. Now we'd reached the other building, and the first door inside was covered with worn leather and embossed with brass nailheads in the form of a cross.

Dan opened it, and Kit pushed me into a dim little vestry. A handmade sign reading LIBRARY was tacked to a door on the left.

I said, "Let's peek in the chapel first."

It was tiny and very devotional, with small, high, stained-glass windows and a flickering red light on the altar making redder the poinsettias there. A very old nun sat in the back pew. She turned and looked at our awkward threesome in the door, smiled, and said, "Please come in."

"Thank you, Sister," I said. "Er—we don't have time. Say a prayer for us."

"I will."

Kit pulled the chair back, and the door swung shut. She pushed me the few feet to the library, and Dan opened the door and groped for a wall switch.

It was even tinier than the chapel—no bigger than my room. There were four straight chairs and a worn sofa, a table with a china lamp, and a bookcase rather sparsely supplied with elderly books.

Dan moved one of the chairs, and Kit pushed me in its place. They sat down, and Dan said to me, "Are you tired? You have to be."

"Dan, come here."

He smiled and came, and I pulled his head down and kissed him and touched the gauze patch in his hair. I said, "He'll pay for this. Did he get the letter?"

"Yes. You should fire me. Keep Kit."

"Sit down and listen to me. You must be in some pain."

"Not a lot, really."

"You will be. Those cuts aren't funny, and I had a broken wrist once. It's awful at night—you can't get comfortable. We'll talk now, then you two are going home. You're both fired."

"But—"

"Dwight Dunlop has his letter, and I'm safe."

"Like hell you are." Dan positioned his cast on the arm of the sofa. "Are you supposed to be happy and trustful of him when you find out what he did to get the damn thing?"

"What *did* he do, actually?"

"Well, he didn't do it himself, that's for sure. It was no seventy-year-old man who jumped me. The guy was young and strong."

The door opened, and Sadd came in with a brown paper parcel in the crook of his arm. A package of plastic glasses was perched precariously on top. Kit got up and took the glasses.

53

Sadd said, "I wanted to get something decent, but I doubted that there was a corkscrew among the chapel artifacts, so I got some tank car with a twist-off top."

"What's tank car?" Kit distributed glasses. "I love your lingo."

"Nice alliteration." Sadd smiled at her. "It's cheap wine that is literally shipped in tanks." He looked around. "What an ideal little hidey-hole. I hope we won't be disturbed. Best keep our voices down." He started to pour.

I said, "Dan is about to tell us what happened."

Kit and Sadd sat down, and Dan looked into his wine.

"I was so sure I'd covered my ass. I took a cab to your door and licked into the vestibule. No sign of Dunlop. Not that I expected him to be obviously hanging around, but I thought he'd at least stroll by and check the place out. Then I realized he'd probably already done that. I figured he'd materialize from some doorway he'd ducked into with the mailman." Dan swirled his wine, then took a sip. "Well, the mail came, but Dunlop didn't."

Sadd got up and topped off my wine, then he sat down, hitching his chair nearer to the bookcase. Despite our irregular, even wacky situation—the four of us huddled in this dim little room and me AWOL—I knew that what Sadd wanted most at that moment was to study those faded book titles.

Dan went on. "I opened the box and saw Mrs. Folsom's letter with her return address on it and put it inside my parka. I let myself in the front door and went up to your place and put the rest of the mail on your desk. I didn't want it to be scattered if he jumped me. Then I called a cab and watched for it from your front window. When it came, I went down and crossed the pavement like a streak. No interference, no nothing. On the way down here I figured he'd heeded Mrs. Folsom's warning and left town. I sat back in the cab feeling good that you weren't in danger anymore."

Poor Dan. He gulped his wine and spilled some, and Kit mopped his front. I bled for him. Mawkish and unprofessional, Clara. He sat up straighter.

"The traffic was backed up on Greenwich Street, so I decided to get out of the cab at Eleventh and take a shortcut through the hospital garage. I went past the ticket booth and up the incline to the first level. Don't ask me where the guy came from. I landed on my face between two cars with a wool cap pulled over my eyes, and he was ripping my parka and frisking me. *Shit!* I'd made it so easy for Dunlop! All he had to do was see me get in that cab and then phone his goon to watch for it at the hospital."

We were silent for a minute, then Kit said, looking at me, "Does this kind of violence mean that he knows you know and he doesn't give a damn?"

"Yes. I think . . ." I suddenly felt cold, though the room was very hot, and shivered and rubbed my knees. Kit was on her feet. "You're going back." She draped Dan's destroyed parka over me.

Dan stood up. "You think what?"

"I think he knew that Janet would panic and come to me."

Sadd said, "You mean before the letter did?"

"Yes. He may even—revolting thought—have hung around here and seen her come. What he's saying now is that he can play rough, maybe rougher, if I don't do what Janet refused to do."

"Deal?" asked Kit, collecting glasses.

"Yes. Look the other way till he can salvage something. He called me this afternoon."

"He called you?" said Dan and Kit together.

"Yes. Very chatty. He's playing business as usual, and he's telling me I'd better do the same."

Sadd, cradling his parcel again, held the door and Kit pushed me through. She said, "How can he be sure you won't go to the police?"

"With what?" I said. "Besides, he knows it would be easier to go to Sal."

As I spoke the words, something began to bug me . . .

I stared out at the night city as we went back down the glass-enclosed passage. The streets were bright with garish colors the way they should be at Christmas. Lights went on in a big, old-fashioned crèche on the hospital grounds as we passed by it. I looked nostalgically at the funny old figures, sheep half the size of the camels, Wise Men looking like children in costume.

Bug me . . .

Why was this man so anxious to get his hands on a letter that had nothing positively incriminating in it? Why risk murder and mugging rather than face the mere railings of an angry woman? I presumed Janet's letter contained only that—mere railings. Surely he'd have a good chance of bluffing his way through with the charm that had always served him so well. Sal adored him. Mightn't she forgive all? Believe in his new leaf? Why had he chosen such a desperate path?

It was puzzling that a scribbled tirade had had the power to put me in this wheelchair.

7

THE ELEVATOR DOOR OPENED ON MY FLOOR
to disclose Henry, Tina, and my ten-year-old grandson,
Hen.

"Where the hell have you been?" My indignant son
helped pull the wheelchair out. I said, "Don't swear in
front of your child," and Hen said, "Can I push?"

I was whisked into my room, fearfully looking about
for D.N. No sign of her—off duty, I hoped. "How long
have you people been here?" I asked.

"It must be all of ten minutes." Tina winked at me as
she and Kit helped me into bed. Hen immediately sat in
the wheelchair and was hauled out of it by his father.
"Henry was sure you'd been abducted."

"You didn't make inquiries, I hope." The thought of
a general alarm and of the dismay of Sister Agnes
equally appalled me.

"Another five minutes, and I would have." Henry
stared at Dan's arm. "My God, did he get to you?"

"He got to me, and he got to the letter." Dan looked
the picture of desolation.

"Dan did fine," I said. "He forced Dwight Dunlop

into the open. Everybody sit. Hen, dear, go into the next room and ask if you may borrow a chair."

"I'll use this one." Sadd sank into the wheelchair. "I'm practically a candidate for it."

"I still want to know where you've been," Henry insisted.

"At a wine-tasting party." Sadd pulled the bottle and glasses from the bag. "Very old stock. Eleventh Street Vineyards. Care for some?"

Henry said come on, what was this all about, and I suddenly felt a little light-headed. I said, "What time is it? I think I'd better eat something."

Everybody asked what I wanted, and I tried to think what I'd had in the course of that long, long day. A piece of French toast and two glasses of wine.

Sadd said, "It's seven o'clock, and I'm absolutely famished. As for Dan and Kit—"

"—as for Dan and Kit"—I looked at them remorsefully—"you are both to go straight down to the cafeteria and have supper. When you've finished, bring me anything."

"Bring me everything," said Sadd, reaching for his wallet.

"It goes on our bill."

Kit and Dan were at the door as Hen returned dragging a chair. He said, "Can I write on your cast?"

"*May* you write," said Sadd.

"Sure," said Dan.

"When my dad broke his arm skiing, people wrote some neat things."

Kit said, "Come down to the cafeteria with us and write a neat thing."

"Can I get some ice cream?"

"May," Sadd said wearily.

"Hen, we've eaten, remember?" said Tina.

"No sweat." Kit put her arm around him. "I have one like you."

"Which reminds me, Kit," I said anxiously, "what's your situation at home?"

"It's okay. My mother lives with us."

They left, and Henry said, "For the third time—"

"Of course, dear, I'm sorry." I lay back, fighting exhaustion. "Sadd, you tell them."

I listened with admiration as Sadd expertly summarized the events from Dwight Dunlop's phone call on. Where I tend to digress, Sadd is concise; I dramatize, he is matter-of-fact; I bewail, he is philosophical.

When he'd finished, Henry said at once, "Of course, Dan's right, Mom. You're not home free."

"It's Janet I'm concerned about," I said.

Tina set her wine glass down. "Pardon me if I sound uncaring about this Janet—not having met her, I can't work up steam about her safety—but what I wish is that we could get *you* out of here, Clara, and back to Nice Ugly."

"Or on a plane to Florida," said Sadd. He rolled the wheelchair to a floor lamp and opened a book.

"What does the doctor say?" asked Henry.

"I don't know. I haven't asked her." My light-headedness was returning. "How long have I been in this place?"

"Since Sunday. This is Tuesday."

I lay with my eyes closed thinking of Janet. I'd promised to call her. Through the door came Sister Agnes with my pill. Henry and Tina hovered at the bed as I got it down.

"How's she doing, Sister?" asked Tina.

"Pretty well," said Sister with all the caution of her calling.

"I've taken enough of these things to tranquilize an elephant," I said. Sister left, and I added, "Dr. Cullen simply can't keep me here over Christmas."

"I'm going to call her." Henry reached for the phone as it rang. He answered, listened for a few seconds, then said, "This is Henry, Janet. My mother's had a rough day. Dwight Dunlop got hold of your letter, so we're concerned about you. . . . Yes, here she is."

He put the receiver in my hand, motioned to Tina to pick up the other one, and said, "I'm going down the hall to a booth. What's Dr. Cullen's number?" I pointed to the pad, and he left. Janet's agitated voice was reaching me from ten inches away, but I ignored it and said without preamble, "Janet, I hope you remember what Dan told you. Stay in your room till—"

"I've checked out of the Plaza, Clara."

"You've gone home?"

"I'm downstairs."

Good God. "Janet! That man is everywhere!"

"I know. It's awful—he almost seems to have bilocation."

"What's bilocation?"

Sadd looked up from his book. "It's the property certain saints are said to have had of being in two places at the same time."

Janet was saying more or less the same thing. I said incredulously, "Saints?"

"And devils," said Janet.

That figured. "Devils, too," I said to Sadd.

He shrugged. "Could be. Fiends are sometimes said to be granted supernatural powers. In *The Screwtape Letters*—"

But it was Janet I was listening to.

"Clara, I've got to see you. Look—I'm going into the flower shop here in the lobby—"

"I don't want any flowers, Janet!"

"—and get some flowers for the chapel." Oops. "Then please let me come up."

"Of course! But stay in the shop till Dan comes for you. He's in the cafeteria, and he'll be back any minute. Don't budge out of there till he comes."

"Okay. But now we have to go to the police."

"With what?" Hadn't I spoken those words recently?

She seemed to hesitate. "Well—with ... something I've got."

Ah. A flicker of light. I said, "Was this 'something' by any chance mentioned in your letter?"

"Yes. It could put him in prison."

"Why didn't you—"

"I know. I should have leveled with you this morning. Well, I will now. See you shortly."

She hung up, and Tina and I did the same. She said, "Do you want me to go down?"

"Maybe." I groaned. "I won't rest till she's in this room. If only Dan and Kit would—"

And at that moment they did, bearing pungent trays. Sadd fell upon his, and Tina said, "Where's my son?"

"He spied his dad in a phone booth down the hall," said Kit.

I said, "Will one or both of you please go down to the flower shop in the lobby? Janet Folsom is there buying flowers for the chapel." They simply gazed at me. "There was a zinger in that letter she neglected to tell us about."

Dan was halfway to the door. "Better come with me, honey. I'm Captain Hook without the hook."

"And by the way"—I drank milk—"you're both rehired—for Janet. But she lives in Connecticut. Can you handle that?"

Dan said, "We could handle Nome, Alaska, for you." Then he grinned and looked down at his cast. "And here's some good advice from your grandson: 'Next time don't be a stupid dope/Look out for the curves and watch the slope.' "

"Fresh kid," said Tina, but she was smiling as we all were.

"Quite a subtle metaphor there," chuckled Sadd. They left, and he added, "And by the way, Clara, *budge out* is redundant. The word *budge* stands alone as meaning—"

"I can't eat any more." I pushed my tray away.

"May I have your roll?" he asked.

"Take it."

"You haven't eaten three bites," scolded Tina. "And you've lost weight already. I can see it in your face."

"Really?" Why is the thought of weight loss so cheering even in the midst of terror and tragedy? "Tina, how much of all this have you told Hen?"

"Not everything. He knows you're involved in a 'situation,' but he's known about your 'situations' since babyhood. We don't want him to know you're in direct danger. He's pretty fond of his gran."

"He is also"—Sadd sipped his coffee—"showing sinister signs of inheriting qualities from both his paternal grandparents such as stubbornness, king-sized curiosity—"

Henry and Hen walked in. Henry said, "Dr. Cullen will be here shortly. She wants to talk to us. I think you may be discharged."

"Lovely!" I cried.

"You'll be home for Christmas, Gran!"

"I know! What are you giving me, by the way?"

Hen considered. "How would you like a board I painted in camp with hooks on it for keys?"

"You gave me one of those last Christmas."

"And I made a rack that holds neckties."

"I don't wear them a lot."

Hen started through his inventory, and Henry turned to Sadd and Tina. "What's this I hear about Janet Folsom? She's *here*?"

As they told him, I began to feel the tiniest kernel of dread forming inside me somewhere. How long since Dan and Kit had gone down? I asked the question aloud, and Tina looked at her watch and guessed fifteen minutes. Sadd closed his book.

"—and I made some place mats," Hen was saying. "One of the kids brought this big book from his father's store. It had pieces of wallpaper in it with—"

"Place mats will be fine, dear." A reassuring thought had occurred to me. The chapel. Janet had probably insisted that they take her to the chapel with her flowers, in which case—

Kit's face, as she opened the door, was white as chalk, but she spoke calmly. "Hen, how would you like to go to the movies?"

"Yeah!"

"I just talked to my mother on the phone." Kit's eyes went from one of us to the other, and she spoke very quietly. "She's taking Danny, and she'd like to take you too. She's coming down in a cab, and she'll go to the side entrance on Tenth Street. Your folks can pick you up later at our house, okay?"

"Okay?" Hen looked eagerly at his parents, and the poor things could only look at Kit, who said in a pleading near-whisper, *"Please?"*

They nodded mutely.

"Neat-o!" Hen darted to the door, and Sadd stood up. "I'll take him down. Tenth Street entrance?"

"Yes. Don't use the elevator. The lobby's . . . er . . . crowded. Take the stairs—turn left out of here, across from the restrooms."

Henry and Tina moved a little. She said, "Hen, stay with Uncle Sadd every minute."

65

Henry said, "Will you give him some money, please, Sadd?"

"Sure thing." Sadd took Hen's hand, and they went out.

"Where?" I heard myself say. "Where?"

"In the chapel." Kit, who hadn't moved from the door, leaned against it. "She'd told the lady in the flower shop there would be somebody asking for her and to please say Mrs. Folsom had gone to the chapel and would be right back."

Strains of "Silent Night" drifted up from that unending source on the street. Henry came to the bed and took my hand. He said, "How, Kit?"

"She was strangled from behind, very expertly. She was slumped over in the front pew. Pocketbook ransacked, of course."

"Who found her?" I think it was Tina's voice.

"Dan and I did."

There was a pause, an empty few seconds, then Kit spoke again. "She was clutching something, and I got it out of her hand. I should have left it, but it looked like something religious and you never know what happens to personal effects in a situation like this. I thought you might like to have it, Mrs. Gamadge."

Kit put something in my frozen hand. Blurrily, I saw that it was two little squares of brown burlap on a string.

8

THE SNOW-PACKED WINDOW WAS THE FIRST thing I became conscious of in the low light of the room, then the presence of both D.N. and Sister Agnes, and then the feeling of being perched on the wretched bedpan.

I said groggily, "What time is it?"

"Two in the morning," said D.N. "Through with the pan?"

"Yes. Why do I feel like this?"

"Dr. Cullen gave you a shot." Sister Agnes spoke very gently. "You said the woman who was murdered in the chapel was a friend of yours, and you were real upset."

Oh, real, *real* upset. I thought idiotically of Sadd's repeated complaint that it should not be *real* but *very*. Sadd. Where was he? Where was the rest of my family? Gone home to bed, idiot. How much do you think they can take?

D.N. started out with her burden. She said, "Your son's here."

Henry came in, his outline in the dimness of the room

67

so like his father's. Sister Agnes said kindly, "Dr. Cullen said he could stay all night, and I'd have let him anyway."

"Sister, you're a saint." Henry smiled at her, and she went out.

"Henry, go home," I said, weeping.

"Are you okay?"

"I'm absolutely and completely okay, and I'd give a million dollars to be able to go to the police."

He shook his head. "Can't yet. There's the small matter of evidence, you know."

I did indeed know, and my heart sank. "We'll get it," I almost shouted, and my head throbbed. "*Why* did I have to have that shot?"

"Because you sort of went to pieces."

"Well, I'm together again, and I'd like some coffee."

"There's a pot at the nurses' station. Be right back."

I lay staring into space, gradually realizing that the dead eye of the television was staring back at me. Should I turn it on and possibly be treated to the sight of Janet's sheeted form being carried out, a prime item on the late-night news? Would it do me any good to see that? Would I benefit from the press's gabby speculations? No. Kit's terse report was all I'd ever need.

Henry came back with the coffee, and I said, "Did Hen get picked up?"

"Yes. Tina and Sadd collected him. He had a great time. Kit said she knew it was a school night, but it was the only way she could think of to get Hen out of here. I consider it inspired."

"So do I." My estimation of Kit soared. Coming up with a quick, clever, humane move under appalling circumstances, she could still regret it being a "school night."

Henry said, "I insisted she and Dan stay home tonight."

"Good. Now, you go home too, dear. Is the snow very bad? I hope you're not driving in this."

"No, Tina has the car. I'll cab it."

"So go."

"Not till Dan comes in at six."

I believe there's an expression that "something snaps inside you." In my case it wasn't so much a snap as a surge of pure rage.

"Henry, I'm sick to death of bodyguards and special food and long-suffering relatives standing by! I almost wish Dwight Dunlop would walk in this room right now. I'd spit in his eye as he killed me—just so you saw him do it." I gulped my coffee. "Damn! I wish I could just *talk* to the police, I mean, in a sort of general way—"

"Mom, you'd never forgive yourself if you tipped your hand. Remember, we have to consider Sal's safety. She's going to be Dunlop's ultimate shield."

"Oh, poor Sal, poor Sal . . ." I realized my voice was trailing. "Why do I feel weird again?"

"It's the shot. Dr. Cullen said it's the kind that will let you come up for a while and then you'll go down again. It's—"

"It's a plot to keep me woozy!" I cried, as indignantly as wooziness would allow.

"Yes, actually." Henry leaned over and kissed me. "We knew you'd be like a raging lion. Don't fight it. See you later."

"Must you sit outside that door?" I murmured, wishing terribly that someone was sitting outside Sal's door . . .

I surfaced to half-light and the snow on the window turning to rain. A young nurse was washing my face, and Dr. Cullen was standing by the bed.

"Mrs. Gamadge, I know you'll be disappointed, but you can't go home just yet."

I glared at her around the facecloth. "What's 'just yet'? Not today?"

"And not tomorrow. You've suffered a severe shock."

"You bet I have. I need to go home and recuperate."

She didn't smile. "You need to stay right here. I promise to let you go on Christmas Eve."

Christmas. Was that still going to happen in the midst of all this horror? I put my hands up and pressed the warm, damp facecloth against my eyes. I said, "I'm in a fog. When's Christmas?"

"Saturday. This is Wednesday."

I looked at the wall. Dear Santa, for Christmas I would like Dwight Dunlop behind bars. The nurse dried my face and left. Dr. Cullen drew a chair to the bed and sat down. Her hand on my pulse, she said, "Your son told me you know who killed your friend but you can't prove it."

"Yes." I turned my head and looked at her. "Were you in the hospital when it happened?"

"No. I was at home. I'd just talked to your son on the phone, and I was coming to the hospital to see another patient, so I said I'd stop by to tell you . . ."

"I could go home."

"Yes. When I got here the police were all over the place. Of course, I didn't connect it with you when they said a woman had been murdered in the chapel."

Murder in the cathedral. I am in no danger, only near to death . . .

She released my wrist and sat back in the chair. "Your son also told me this man is the same one who tried to kill you."

"Yes."

"And that you know a woman who is more or less hostage to him."

"Yes."

"And of course you yourself are still a threat to him."

"Yes."

The door opened, and Dan put his head in. "Want some breakfast?"

"No, thanks."

He smiled at Dr. Cullen and closed the door.

She stood up. "I'd do anything in the world to help."

"Thank you. For one thing, you can let me dispense with the bedpan."

"Okay. If you'll be careful and let a nurse help you up."

"And don't jab me with any more of that sleep stuff."

"Promise." She squeezed my hand. "You'll probably

71

doze off once more. I've stopped all calls till noon. You'll be fine by then."

"And if you *really* want to help, you can let me go home today."

She smiled and walked to the door. "I don't believe I've told you that my father was a New York City police officer."

"Really?"

"Believe me, you're a lot safer here than you would be at home."

I said ungraciously, "Is that the police officer's daughter speaking or the doctor in cahoots with my family?"

Now she laughed. "Some of both."

Dr. Cullen was right; I woke up refreshed and hungry. Lunch trays rattled in the hall. I hobbled to the bathroom—the heck with the nurse—hobbled back to bed, and was pouring myself the last of Sadd's tank car when Dan came in with steaming soup and a salad.

"Wonderful," I said, tackling the soup. "Dan, we need a conference."

"Yes. Henry and Kit are both coming in."

He went out, and I settled back to answer a series of five phone calls in quick succession.

Henry's was the first. "You sound better, Mom. I hope I didn't upset you further by emphasizing Sal's danger."

"Of course not, dear. If I hadn't been so punchy, I'd

have realized it sooner. It's frustrating—but no police yet."

"Meanwhile you can work on Do It Yourself. You've done it before."

"But I'm stuck here till Christmas Eve! Dr. Cullen won't let me out! Do I detect your fine hand—"

"Look—lie back and play Nero Wolfe. We'll all play Archie. We might even bring you orchids. See you later."

Second call. "Mrs. Gamadge, this is Kit. Are you okay? Can you handle some brainstorming this afternoon?"

"I sure can. And speaking of handling things—thanks for last night."

"Hen and Danny hit it off great. Be seeing you."

Third call. "Clara, I'm mad and jealous."

"Why, Tina?"

"Because Henry is taking today and tomorrow off, and he and Kit and Dan will be huddling with you, and I'm stuck in the office. Er—one more thing. Sal just called me."

My mouth went a little dry. "At the office?"

"Yes. She said she'd tried the hospital and you weren't allowed calls this morning and she had an awful feeling she knew why. You'd heard about that woman who was murdered, and she was a friend of both of yours, and you were probably devastated."

"What did you say?"

"I said yes, you certainly were devastated, and it would be best if she not try to call you right away."

"Bless you, Tina."

73

The fourth caller was Sadd. "Have you pulled your-self together?"

"I was never apart," I said indignantly.

"I almost was. After I delivered Hen to Kit's mother, I walked back toward the chapel, and I wish I hadn't. They were carting your poor friend out."

"Oh, God, Sadd, why did you go near the place?"

"I didn't go near it—I wasn't allowed to. Actually, all I wanted to do was duck in that little library. I saw a book there yesterday I wanted to borrow."

Death and disaster strike, and Sadd wants to borrow a book.

He went on, "I'm on my way over. Shall I stop at your place and get the mail?"

"Oh, Sadd, would you? I've been such a nuisance to everybody, I didn't dare ask."

"Let's hope I don't suffer the same fate as the last person who opened your box."

The fifth call was from Paula. Mercifully, news of the murder in St. Victor's Hospital in New York hadn't reached Boston. We chatted, she rejoiced at my prog-ress, and we agreed she'd bring the family to New York for Christmas.

I hung up, pulled my salad forward, and reached for the fork. At the third bite the sixth call came. "Clara, this is Dwight. Feeling better?"

Down went the fork, and up came the bite. He went on briskly, "I'll try to be brief because I know you've been under strain, but it's important that we understand each other before you make any wrong moves."

I found my voice. "You're making one now. I'm not alone."

"Of course you're alone. I just walked past your door. I'm in the booth down the hall."

9

IT WAS HIS PROXIMITY, HIS CLOSE, CALM, creepy proximity that filled me with horror. Not fear. I felt almost no fear, only horror—then rage at the deadly arrogance of the man.

He went on matter-of-factly, "That young man outside your door with the cast on his arm—I presume he's watching out for you? Glad to hear it. Now, Clara, regarding the point that I'm sure has been disturbing you most, you may put your mind at ease. I'm leaving New York on Christmas Day. I won't be back. Ever. That's a promise."

"Good God!" broke from me. "A promise from *you*?"

He ignored this outburst. "I'm glad I'm leaving Sal in good hands. I've grown very fond of her. She'll need lots of support and consolation, and I'm sure you'll—"

"It's a pity"—I made my voice steady—"that Janet Folsom isn't here to help with support and consolation."

"Who? Oh, you mean that poor woman who was murdered in the hospital? Wasn't that ghastly? We heard about it on the late news, and Sal said you both

76

knew her. We assumed she was there to see you, which must make you feel doubly bad. Really, New York is getting worse and worse. I'll be glad to get out of it."

My stomach turning, I said, "Will you take all of Sal's money when you go, or will you leave her enough to keep the store?"

He sighed. "Unfortunately, having to leave so precipitously, I'll only be able to avail myself of—"

"—lay your hands on—"

"—the Christmas cash. But it will tide me over." His voice became businesslike. "Now, Clara, listen to me carefully. If you in any way attempt to contact the police or prevent me from leaving, or hint at anything to Sal, it will be the worse for her. You must keep that firmly in mind."

And this creature was standing fifty feet from me and Dan! Oh, where was a shred of evidence that would enable me to leap from my bed shrieking, "Murderer!" I told myself not to be dramatic, and as he went on I only half listened. Defeat and anger. That's what I must project. He must believe that I feel licked. He was saying, "—and we have a great idea for the store on Christmas Eve. Punch and cookies in the children's section, and yours truly will be Santa. I can't wait! I rented the costume yesterday."

The utter desecration of it. I said, "Dwight—since that's the only name I know you by—"

"An elegant one, don't you think? I like it the best. And I was a great admirer of President Eisenhower."

"Since you appear to hold all the cards, I guess the

77

only thing I can say, with all my heart, is this: go to hell—literally."

"Now, don't be a poor loser, Clara. You're a delightful lady, and I've enjoyed my dealings with you. In fact, I'd like to think I've been one of your greatest challenges."

"Oh, you are, you are."

"*Have been,* Clara, *have been.* It's all in the past, or will be in a few days. You mustn't forget that, for Sal's sake and possibly for your own, and—er—your family's. Well, back to the store."

He was gone, and I sat stupefied, then called shrilly, "Dan!" He appeared. "Dwight Dunlop is just leaving the hospital headed for Cornelia Street."

"What?"

"No time to explain. See if you can follow him!"

"I've never seen him!"

"I know. I want you to—so you can identify him—a big, tall, fleshy man—maybe you'd better dash ahead to Pushing Murder and wait for him. Don't let him see you—he'll recognize your cast. There's a coffee shop across the street—wait there. I want to be sure he does go back to the store."

"I don't under—"

"No need to—go!"

"Who'll cover you?"

"Mr. Saddlier's on his way up—go!"

He darted off, and I sat breathing like a superannuated runner. I'd gotten rid of Dan briefly, but did I still have time? . . . I reached for my watch on the bedside cabinet, and my hand encountered something small and rough. Janet's scapular. I examined it for the first time. There were two squares, each imprinted with the image of the saint and connected with a double length of tape, one square apparently worn in front and the other in back. I stared at it. St. Benedict. How was he on miracles? That seemed about our only hope at this point.

A hospital volunteer, Mrs. Ling, pleasant, middle-aged, and Chinese, came in with newspapers. I hadn't looked at one since I'd landed here, but now I took a tabloid and the *New York Times*.

"Isn't this murder terrible?" she said in the perfect English that both amazes and mortifies nonlinguists like myself. "One of the nurses has told me you were a friend of this woman."

"Yes, terrible. And yes, she was a friend."

Mrs. Ling shook her head sympathetically and withdrew. I gritted my teeth and flipped past the tabloid headline WOMAN SLAIN ON ALTAR STEPS to page two, where I read that "broken blossoms were strewn about the body of a woman identified as Mrs. Janet Folsom, Fairfield, Connecticut, socialite," who was apparently in the act of "laying her floral tribute on the altar of St. Victor's Hospital chapel when she was strangled and robbed." The police had no lead on the killer.

The *Times* eschewed what Sadd calls "that awful word *socialite*" and called Janet Folsom a "wealthy and respected philanthropist." Only two relatives were named, a sister-in-law, Mrs. Loretta Vaughan, also of Fairfield, and an uncle of her late husband, Reverend Robert Folsom, a Benedictine priest.

The sister-in-law I knew slightly. The clerical uncle I'd not been aware of.

I folded the newspapers and pressed my buzzer. To my relief, Sister Agnes appeared. I'd better get the boss's permission this time, my team of conspirators not being present.

I said, "Sister, would it be possible to have an aide or a volunteer take me down to the chapel in the wheel-chair?"

She looked doubtful. "Mrs. Gamadge—"

"I feel the need of a little spiritual consolation." I tried to look the need, and it wasn't hard.

"Father McCarthy will be making rounds this afternoon."

"That will be lovely, but I'd just like to say a prayer in the place where my poor friend died."

"I'm not sure they'll let you in. I understand the police have closed the chapel temporarily."

"In that case I'll come straight back. Please?" *Please.* I was not up for another secret flight, but if worst came to worst . . .

She smiled and relented. "If you promise not to stay too long."

"Promise!"

"I'll ask Mrs. Ling to take you down. She's probably through with her papers." Sister went to the closet. "As well as your robe, I want a blanket over your knees. The chapel is all the way in the next building."

"Is it?" I said innocently.

"I'll remind Mrs. Ling how to get there." I restrained myself. "Now, remember—"

"Just a quick prayer."

Ten minutes later Mrs. Ling and I emerged from an elevator beside the chapel sign and beheld, as I'd hoped we would, a half-dozen or so policemen, any one of whom might have recognized Dan. Now I was just an anonymous old lady in a wheelchair milling with the crowd.

"Officer," I quavered to a stocky one nearby, "I would so love to visit the chapel, but I understand there's been something awful—a murder?"

"Yes, ma'am. The chapel's closed to the public to-day."

"Oh, dear. Do you suppose I could speak—I mean, is there someone in charge?"

"That's Captain Redmond right there." He took three steps to a wiry, gray-haired officer. Ah! Captain Redmond. The horse's mouth? Mrs. Ling pushed me to a place near the wall, remarking on the crowd and hoping it wasn't going to be too much for me. Captain Redmond was approaching.

"What can I do for you, ma'am?"

"Oh, Captain, I did so want to say a prayer in the chapel. You see—"

Helpful Mrs. Ling interrupted in that fatally good English of hers. "Captain, this lady is a friend of the woman who was murdered."

So much for carefulness. I heard my son's voice: "You'd never forgive yourself if you tipped your hand. . . . Consider Sal's safety. . . ."

Captain Redmond was looking at me with interest. He said, "A friend, now. Is that so?"

"Well, I knew her slightly." I adjusted the blanket over my knees, avoiding his eyes. "Do you have any leads?"

"I'm afraid not." The captain's eyes were definitely *not* avoiding mine. "May I have your name, ma'am?"

"Clara Gamadge."

"Maybe you know why the victim was here. Maybe to visit you?"

"That's a possibility, and it makes me feel just awful. Well, I'm a little tired so perhaps I'll skip—"

"You're welcome to visit the chapel." He was graciousness itself. "We just want to keep out the curious. I'll go with you."

"I really shouldn't keep Mrs. Ling from—"

"I don't mind at all." She was all solicitude. "And you said you were most anxious."

Between graciousness and solicitude I was trapped. But keep your mouth shut, Clara. Janet Folsom was a chance acquaintance, and I had no connection with her presence here. Captain Redmond walked with us as Mrs. Ling pushed my chair down the glass corridor. I felt as if Dwight Dunlop stalked beside me and arrived with us at the leather door. Had he followed Janet, or had he waited for her? The captain nodded to a patrolman, who opened the door, and we entered the vestry. As the door started to close behind us, Sadd's voice said, "May I come in too?"

We turned, and I said quickly, "This is my cousin Charles Saddlier—Captain Redmond, Sadd." *Don't* let Sadd say they'd told him upstairs I'd gone to say a prayer for my dear friend Janet Folsom.

Sadd indicated the library sign. "Not exactly a branch of the NYPL, but I saw a book I wanted to borrow when I was here yesterday."

"Yesterday?" said the captain. "What time would that have been?"

I sneezed noisily, and Mrs. Ling produced a tissue.

"Oh, quite early, before all the excitement. Well"— Sadd edged toward the library—"I hope the book is in and there isn't a waiting list for it." He smiled feebly and disappeared.

Captain Redmond held open the chapel door. A half-dozen persons, including two police officers, sat in pews or stood in the aisle, and video equipment lay about. The sun must have emerged from clouds at that moment, for the vivid old windows on one side of the chapel lit up as if controlled by a heavenly dimmer and a reddish glow bathed the transept.

Captain Redmond leaned over and said in my ear, "This is mostly press. If anyone speaks to you, I wouldn't mention knowing the victim or you'll be swamped."

Captain, you read my mind. I nodded and tried to look grateful, though I had an uneasy feeling he was saving me for himself alone. Mrs. Ling pushed me down the aisle and asked if I wanted to be helped into a pew. I said no, I'd just sit here for a minute or two. Was this left front pew where the—the woman was found? No, the captain said, it was the right one.

He walked back down the aisle, and Mrs. Ling slid into another pew. I sat contemplating the shiny wooden seat, the ramrod-straight back, the low kneeling bench.

I envisioned the "broken blossoms" and Janet slumped here clutching her scapular. I thought gratefully of Kit extricating it for me. I was glad it was lying in my drawer upstairs and not amid the contents of Janet's pocketbook, being pawed over . . .

Why, oh, why had I come? Or why couldn't some non-English-speaking broom pusher have brought me down? I stared at the altar, which was bare of the flowers that should adorn it. Something else was missing—the little red light that had flickered there yesterday.

Captain Redmond had come back up the aisle and was squatting beside my chair. He said, "Pretty altar, isn't it?"

"Yes." I roused myself and tried to think of something innocuous to say. "But where's the little light?"

"Light?"

Clara, you fool! "Er—yes, I peeked in here once before, and there was a pretty red light on the altar." I started to turn my chair, and Mrs. Ling stood up.

"That would have been the Sanctuary Lamp," said the captain. "It means the Blessed Sacrament is in the tabernacle. The Sisters took it away when all hell broke loose yesterday. When did you say you were here?"

"Oh, quite a while ago." We started down the aisle, and my lie flew up to the sacred rafters and bounced back in my face.

Through the door came an elderly nun. She smiled and nodded, then said, "Aren't you the lady who was here yesterday in the wheelchair? I remember that pretty white hair of yours. And to think it was less than an hour before that poor woman was killed!"

84

And as if that wasn't enough, the door opened again, and Dan stood there. "Oh, hi, Captain Redmond."

"Hello, Dan. What brings you here?"

10

MORTIFIED AND EXHAUSTED, I WAS ASSISTED back into bed by Kit and a scolding Sister Agnes, who said I'd tired myself and she didn't think I should let that policeman talking to my son in the hall come in and tire me further. I groaned and said it was the last thing I wanted anyway.

Sadd, reading by the window, said, "There's a well-worn quotation about practicing to deceive."

Sister Agnes checked my temperature, said that all my prayers were to be uttered in bed from now on, and left.

Straightening my pillows, Kit said, "I don't know why you're so hung up on when we were in the chapel. We didn't even know Folsom was coming back at that point. We just went down to see Dan."

"And Dan had just gotten mugged because of Folsom." I was weakly belligerent. "And I was desperate to disassociate myself from her. Now, thanks to Mrs. Ling and a sweet old nun, I'm a liar and Captain Redmond is breathing down my neck." I reached for my water decanter. "I hope Henry and Dan aren't out there spilling the rest of the beans."

"No." Kit took the glass from me. "They know you want Dunlop kept out of it for now. But they can't deny that Folsom's murder and your attempted one are possibly connected."

"Possibly. I'll give the captain *possibly* but no more."

"Shall I let them in?"

"Give me five minutes." I settled myself grimly. "Then you may open the door of the cage. The lion tamer will be ready with her chair. And Kit"—she turned at the door—"get hold of a Fairfield, Connecticut, phone book. I want to know if Loretta Vaughan is in it."

"She is. Dan looked her up."

She went out, and Sadd stood up. "Your mail is on the table beside you."

"Thanks." I glanced at it without interest.

"Do you want me to stay?"

"I want you to go back to Florida. You've been a pal."

He looked out the window. "And leave this platitudinously lovely white Christmas? The snow has stopped, it's a beautifully bright afternoon, and the streets are clear. I'm tempted to take a walk."

"Why don't you? Henry and I used to love to walk around the Village." I felt the old pang.

He turned from the window. "Maybe I'll stroll up to Cornelia Street."

"Sadd! And drop in on Pushing Murder?"

"Why not? I haven't done any Christmas shopping yet."

"Wonderful!" I started to hug my knees but couldn't.

"Chat with Dwight as if everything were hunky-dory—"

"I have never been able to discover the origin of that phrase."

"—even though he must know you know everything. We have to keep him assured that Sal will remain oblivious."

"In her fool's paradise." Sadd pulled on the dear, familiar parka. "Except that she's no fool, which makes it worse."

He went out, announcing to my visitors as he passed them that he was going to "stretch his legs."

Henry, Dan, and Kit filed in, followed by Captain Redmond, and I said immediately, "Captain, I apologize for fibbing to you. I'm just scared to death for a friend of mine."

"I can understand that, Mrs. Gamadge."

They all sat down, and I played hostess. "I'd love a cup of coffee. Would anyone else?"

No, no one would. Henry went out, and the hostess rattled on. "So you know Dan and Kit."

"Sure do." The captain smiled. "I've been kidding Dan about that cast. A sharp-shooting New York boy like him getting mugged." He went on, looking not at me but at them. "You've got a couple of smart kids watching out for you, Mrs. Gamadge."

"Don't I know it."

The captain crossed his legs and looked back at me. "Your son tells me you've been involved in a certain amount of crime yourself."

"I've dabbled," I murmured. "It was mostly my husband . . ."

"Then you know that the bottom line is evidence. Do you have any evidence in the Folsom murder?"

"Not a shred."

"Just a hefty suspicion?"

"Yes."

"Can I persuade you to share—"

"No. Please. No."

He hesitated. "I can't pressure you, Mrs. Gamadge. You aren't a witness and for all I know you may be on the wrong track."

"Yes, yes, I may be," I said eagerly.

"But you don't really think so, do you?" he said. I squirmed. "How will you feel if this person kills again?"

"He won't, as long as I keep my mouth shut."

"Do you have to keep it shut forever?"

"No. Just till Saturday."

He looked at me steadily. "At which point he will take off, and you and your friend will be safe from him—you hope."

"Something like that," I said uncomfortably. "But believe me, Captain, we'll work night and day to put you on his trail. He has a long record, and with the evidence we're trying for—"

"We could help with that, you know."

"Of course you could, but I don't dare risk it."

Henry had returned with my coffee and handed it to me. "Captain," he said, "the hostage my mother is trying to protect is all unsuspecting. Our man isn't going to budge from her side till he splits for good."

"Is it his wife?"

I said nothing. This game of Twenty Questions was getting too warm. Time to play tired old lady. I lay back wearily.

The captain stood up looking awkward and annoyed. He said, "You know enough about criminal law, Mrs. Gamadge, to realize that there's something called *obstructing justice* which—"

"But I'm doing everything in my power to bring justice about!"

"It may not be enough."

"But then, it may, it may!" I forgot weary and sat forward. "And I promise you just as soon—"

"Did you know that Folsom was checked into the Plaza?"

The question was so unexpected that I floundered. "I know—that is—I know she lives—lived in Connecticut."

"The Plaza receipt was in her pocketbook, but the electronic door card wasn't."

Dunlop had taken it! I said, inanely, "Robbery."

The captain shook his head. "You don't have to kill a woman to rob her. No, more likely blackmail. We went to the room, and there were signs of a search—but then, you probably know that."

Weary time again. "Captain, do you mind if I don't talk anymore? I'm just a wee bit tired."

He held out his hand. "Take care of yourself. When will they let you go home?"

"Christmas Eve, I hope." I pressed his hand gratefully. "May I ask you something?"

He grinned. "Sure you're not just a wee bit tired?"

My gang laughed, and I ignored them. "Do you know who the beneficiaries are?"

"Her lawyer told me off the record that all Folsom's money goes to her charities. Her next of kin are an old priest and a sister-in-law who's richer than she was. They both live in Fairfield, and I'll be paying them a call."

I said, "Captain, you're a good sport, and I'm hoping to give you the biggest, fattest Christmas present you ever got."

"Thanks. I just hope it doesn't cost you your life."

He went out, and I exploded. "Dunlop took the door card!"

"No, he didn't," said Dan. "I did." He held it aloft.

Henry and I stared, and Kit smiled smugly. "No flies on *that* cast."

I said, "Dan—how?"

He tucked it back in his wallet. "While Kit was prying loose that thing in Folsom's hand—what's it called?—"

"Scapular."

"—I dug in the pocketbook fast. I was pretty sure he'd have grabbed any cash—he had—and a room key if he saw one. But I guess Dunlop hasn't been in any class joints lately because he apparently didn't recognize the card as a key. Anyway, it was still there, and while Kit was phoning the police I was in a cab to the Plaza. There wasn't much in the room, just clothes and a couple of books. I left a few drawers open hoping the police would figure robbery, but Redmond's no dope. When I got back to the hospital, one of the cops—a guy I know—said, 'Your wife found a body while you were resting on your ass—I mean your cast.'"

We laughed, and Dan took something from his pocket. He said, "I did lift this because I thought you'd like to have it."

He handed me a worn little black leather prayer book bristling with cards picturing saints and other devotional graphics. One caught my eye and made me gag: a white-robed angel guiding a child away from a precipice. On it was written, "For Janet, herself a guardian angel. Allen, May 1965."

Bastard. I closed the book and laid it beside the scapular.

I said, "Sadd's gone up to Pushing Murder to do some shopping and imply to Dwight that we're playing the game with him."

"I went last night," said Kit. "Your friend Sal is a sweetheart. Dunlop never lets her out of his sight. He showed me his Santa Claus costume and said to bring my son on Christmas Eve."

"In the words of Sheridan Whiteside," I said, "I may vomit."

"Exactly how long do we have?" Henry asked.

Dan looked at his watch. "This is Wednesday. So the rest of today and forty-eight hours."

"It sounds so much less when you say hours," I complained.

"Two and a half days," said Kit consolingly.

Grim silence. Then I said, "I want to talk to Loretta Vaughan and that priest uncle of Janet's. Do you have the number, Dan?" He nodded and opened a notebook.

"Do you know them?" asked Henry.

"I've never met him and I haven't seen her in years. I wish I knew more about them."

Dan looked at his pad. "The priest, Father Robert Folsom, is almost ninety and lives in Mrs. Vaughan's home at 5 Cobb Road, in Fairfield, the same house she's lived in since her marriage in 1950. Her husband died twenty years ago, and she still partly manages the business, which is plastics. *Partly* because of what I'll tell you in a minute. She's horrified at what has happened to her sister-in-law; she remembers Clara Gamadge very well and would rather talk to her than to the police. I said you were in the hospital, and she said she hoped it was nothing serious, and I said it wasn't. She said that she and 'Father Bob,' as she called him, would be happy to come to the hospital any time you say. Morning would be the best because she has a drinking problem and—I quote—'must arrange to be sober.' "

Three pairs of admiring eyes gazed at Dan as he handed me the pad. I looked at my watch. "Three o'clock. She's well in her cups, but I can't wait." I reached for the phone.

"Oh," said Dan, "she added that if she was unable to talk to you, Father Bob would, but that he's a little deaf."

I suppressed a groan, punched numbers, and Kit giggled.

93

"Don't knock it," said Henry. "Ninety and deaf but sober could be more help than drunk at any age."

The phone receiver was lifted, and an extremely pleasant, clear voice said, "Father Folsom speaking."

"Father, this is Clara Gamadge. I was a friend of poor Janet's."

"Yes, Mrs. Gamadge, we understood you might call. This is a terrible shock, and you're in the hospital, which makes it worse for you."

I flashed a triumphant look at my cohorts and said gratefully, "It's ghastly for all of us. I believe Dan—the young man who talked to Loretta—told her I'd had some experience with criminal investigation."

"Yes, Loretta mentioned that. I found it quite extraordinary. In fact, I wasn't sure that she—er—got it right."

"She did."

"And she also said you'd like us to come see you."

"I'd appreciate it."

"Then of course we will. Loretta's secretary, a charming girl, is an excellent driver. She lives in New York and goes back and forth quite often. When shall we come? Mornings are best because"—the pleasant voice grew dejected—"by late afternoon Loretta is usually—shall we say—under the weather."

"Could you come tomorrow as early as possible?"

"Nine o'clock?"

"Wonderful. You know St. Victor's Hospital?"

"Oh, yes. I left my appendix there about a hundred years ago."

We laughed, and I said, "One more thing: please say nothing of this call to anyone."

"Oh, we live very quietly. There's nobody—"

"I mean, if someone should call, perhaps someone you haven't heard from in years—"

"Mrs. Gamadge"—a little laugh—"at my age calls from old friends are a rarity—in fact, old friends themselves are a rarity!"

What a sweetheart. But I had to be definite. "Father, I don't want to sound melodramatic, but please, between now and when I see you, tell no one that I called or that you're coming here."

"If you say so."

"Thanks. See you tomorrow."

I hung up, and Henry said, "Why all the caution? Aren't they a bit remote?"

"How do I know if they're remote?" I kicked at my covers irritably. "How do I know if Dwight even knew them? Maybe he didn't. Maybe he did. And if he did, suppose one of them knows something damaging that wasn't in Janet's letter? And suppose he decides to check on who *I'm* checking on. . . . We don't want him paying them a surprise Christmas visit, do we? Now go home, all of you, and come back tomorrow at nine to meet our visitors."

I dozed, which was a mistake. Bad dreams can be more lethal during an hour's nap than in the course of a whole night. I woke up drenched in misery to find Sadd standing by the bed. His words didn't help a bit.

"The store is a little gem, business is good, and Sal is probably the happiest woman in New York City."

11

"I'M GETTING QUITE ATTACHED TO THIS room," I said at eight forty-five next morning. "I may set up an office here."

I'd been fed, tended, told I was in good shape, and now looked around at fresh floral tributes, more funny cards, and my teammates sipping coffee. "Who's going down to meet our visitors?"

"I will," said Kit, putting down her cup. She left, and I said, "Sadd, tell Dan and Henry about the situation at Pushing Murder."

Sadd put a marker in his book. "Well, he guards her like a dragon. Never leaves her side. I asked her to let me buy her a drink at the corner pub while Dwight minded the store, and she said fatuously that he never let her out of his sight—how right she is—that he was positively jealous and wasn't that silly and wonderful?"

We looked at each other wordlessly. Finally Henry said, "Have they moved into the apartment upstairs yet?"

"Yes, it's just finished, and we're all to be invited for a house-warming after Christmas."

Oh, Lord, oh, Lord.

"As far as I can see," Sadd went on, "they never leave the place. They eat up in the apartment, the phone rings there and in the store—Dunlop leaps for it—all shopping is apparently done in tandem, and Sal loves it."

Dan said, "Did you talk to Dunlop?"

"Yes, indeed. We chatted, and he looked me in the eye, that is, when he wasn't looking at Sal—his vigilance is terrible—and he helped me pick out that stuff." Sadd indicated a red plastic bag with the Pushing Murder logo. "Divide it up. Merry Christmas."

Henry said, "He has to have some weakness, some vulnerability. Does he drink? See other women?"

"He sure as hell won't do either between now and Christmas," said Dan. "The strain on him has got to be awful."

"If it is," I said, "he just keeps saying to himself, 'Only X more hours and I'm free.' Then, in his Santa Claus costume, up the chimney he goes, and dash away, dash away."

There was a tap on the door, and our visitors walked in with Kit.

For someone who had to "arrange" to be sober, Loretta Vaughan looked remarkably well. I remembered her as a big woman and had expected to see ravages, but she was heftier than ever, her gray hair was well groomed, and her gaze direct. Only her hands gave her away. As she took my outstretched one in both of hers, I felt as if I had grasped a live wire. She withdrew them quickly, thrust the poor, vibrating things in the pocket of her coat and said, "Clara, I'm sorry to see you here. And this is Father Bob."

Tiny, bald, and birdlike, his clerical collar engulfing his chin, Father also extended his hand. It was paper thin but firm, and he said, "Mrs. Gamadge, I hope you're better."

I assured him I was and introduced everyone. Loretta kept her hands in her pockets this time and nodded genially around. Father Bob shook hands, and Henry divested him of a dark green parka which would have nicely fit Hen. Loretta shrugged out of her coat, a worn tweed, and said she'd keep it over her shoulders. The lapels, I noticed, were a good grasping ground. Everybody sat down, coffee was offered and accepted.

"Just half a cup for me," said Loretta. Wise. A full cup in those hands would be disastrous.

I said, "You are both wonderful to come."

"We were glad to," said Father. He put up his hand and adjusted a rather prominent hearing aid. "But it's for such a terrible reason."

Loretta looked at the floor. "We're finding this very difficult to believe. It's a relief to talk about it, especially to people who won't gossip and only want to help. But before we say another word, Clara, what's put you in the hospital?"

I'd expected the question and had decided to withhold the whole answer for now. "I broke my ankle. Tell us, where will Janet be buried?"

"She'll be cremated," said Father, "and I'll say a Requiem Mass for her at St. Francis Seminary. Her ashes will go in the family plot in Greenwich, where Lewis is buried."

I reached for the prayer book and the scapular. "Thanks to Kit and Dan, we were able to salvage these. Would either of you like to have them?"

Loretta stood up and took the items from me. She glanced at them and handed them to the priest.

"Your department, Father."

He looked at them, and his thin face worked. "I gave her both."

The poor man. Had I made things worse? But I was trying to ease my way toward the fateful question. I said, "Look at the card with the guardian angel. Does that name mean anything to either of you?"

Loretta leaned toward him as he held it up. Father said, "Of course. May God forgive him."

Loretta sat back in her chair. "What does that SOB have to do with anything?"

Everyone suppressed a smile, and Father Bob said gently, "Retta, there's no call for—"

"—for anything but to wish him in hell—if he isn't already there. Why do you ask, Clara? Are you going to tell us that that pismire has surfaced again?"

"Yes."

"In relation to Janet?"

"Yes."

"My God."

"Retta"—Father looked distressed—"if you're going to be vulgar and profane—"

"—and not even drunk, think what I'll be later." Her hands came out of hiding and rose, shaking, to push the neat gray bangs from her forehead. "Maybe you don't remember as well as I do, Father, but—"

"Certainly I do." The frail shoulders moved. "Who has more reason to remember than I do?"

Sadd has a gift for easing a tense situation by introducing a subject entirely different but somehow apropos. He said, "Father, I have a confession to make. It has to do with your beautiful monastery in Italy, Monte Cassino."

The little priest looked at him in surprise. "Monte Cassino? It was destroyed during the war, you know."

"Yes, and I helped destroy it. I was in the Fifth Army. Mea culpa."

"But you had no choice!" Father Bob was earnest. "It was a Nazi stronghold. The Benedictines had been driven out. And it's been beautifully restored." He smiled. "Absolved."

We all laughed a little except Loretta, who was still staring at the floor. This was all very well, but back to rotten old business. I took the plunge. "Not only has Allen Quinn surfaced—under another name, of course—but he is the man we want."

They both stared at me, and Loretta moistened her lips. "What do you mean?"

"He killed Janet."

She didn't move. Father Bob seemed to shrivel in his chair. Henry stood up and opened my cabinet. He poured sherry into plastic glasses and said, "This will help."

He put it into the priest's hand, but Loretta waved it away and opened her pocketbook. She took out a small flask, uncorked it, and downed the contents in one long pull. She jammed the cork back on and said, "That's all I brought with me, so have no fear that I'll disgrace you. Clara, how do you know this?"

I hesitated. "It's a longish story. He tried to kill me first. That's why I'm here."

Neither spoke. My words seemed incomprehensible to them, and no wonder. I was handling it badly; I was trying to bring two persons in a canoe alongside a torpedo boat. Slow down, Clara, or they'll capsize.

Again Sadd came to the rescue. "Here's what happened: Janet ran into him quite by accident about a week ago. He is going under the name Dwight Dunlop, and he is victimizing a woman—"

"What else?" murmured Father Bob dazedly.

"—whom Janet knew and was fond of. Clara also knows her. Perhaps you do too, Mrs. Vaughan."

I said, "Loretta, do you remember Sara Orne?"

"No. Yes. Vaguely." Loretta looked longingly at her empty flask.

Dan said, "If we can get protection for this woman, we can let the police move in on Dunlop."

"Move in on him!" Loretta glared around. "That sounds as if you know where he is!"

"We do," I said.

"Clara—with my bare hands—"

"Retta"—the priest touched his ear with a trembling hand but spoke firmly—"we're here to help. You're not doing it with this exhibition."

The door opened, and an aide came in with a magnificent poinsettia. Kit found a place for it and handed me

101

the card. I put it aside, and Loretta said, "Okay, okay, you want to protect this person. I suppose I can understand that. But how in heaven's name can we help? After thirty years, he's well in the clear on the St. Elizabeth episode."

"But there were other episodes," said Henry. "And one might lead to another. Were you ever able to garner the smallest scrap of information on him since?"

Loretta was shaking her head grimly and thrusting the flask back in her pocket. "Not the smallest scrap. And believe me, Janet left no stone unturned. He became a second Invisible Man."

"The first one was traced," said Sadd thoughtfully, "partly by his footprints in the snow. We're hoping Allen Quinn left some footprints."

Loretta looked at him. "What's that name he's going by now?"

"Dwight Dunlop."

She snorted. "Of all the phony, pretentious—"

"There were other names in between," I said.

"I'll bet there were!"

Dan said, "And you have no records or documents or correspondence pertaining to him?"

"None." It was Father Bob who spoke now, rousing himself. "When St. Elizabeth's closed, that chapter of Janet's life closed, and she never spoke of him again. And she never went to Bryantville again."

"Where?" said Loretta, looking at him blankly. Then, "Oh, was that the name of the town? I can't even remember where it was."

Kit said, "Mrs. Folsom said central Connecticut."

102

"Probably." Loretta's hands found refuge in her coat pockets, no doubt clasping the comforting flask. "Yes—now that I think of it, Janet had found some place out in the boonies, in the Waterbury area."

"Did you ever know anybody in the town?" asked Dan.

Loretta looked as astonished as if she'd been asked if she knew someone in Outer Mongolia.

Father Bob said, "Actually, there was one sad little last incident." He took a sip of his sherry. "Remember the girl from Bryantville who came to see us, Retta?"

Again she looked blank, then nodded. "Sure. Forgot about her."

"It was a month or two after Allen disappeared." Father Bob looked into his glass. "She came to Janet in a distraught condition, saying she was expecting his child. We had no reason not to believe her."

"No reason *whatever*," said Loretta.

"But what could we do but help her financially?" He took another sip as we all sat rather still. A child who would now be what?—middle twenties?

Kit said, "And was it—was the child ever born?"

"I haven't the foggiest." Loretta looked at her watch. "We never saw the girl again. Janet may have. It would be like her."

"Do you remember her name?" asked Dan.

They looked at each other helplessly, then Father passed his hand over his eyes. "It's all so long ago . . ."

"It was the usual sordid story." Loretta stood up. "Of course he'd promised to marry her, and of course she didn't know he was already married."

"Married?" Five spoke as one.

"To who?" I said.

"Whom," said Sadd.

They looked at each other in surprise.

"To Janet, of course," said Father Bob.

Stunned silence, then I got out the words. "And Janet never divorced him?"

"Never."

"He's a bloody bigamist!" cried Dan.

Of course. That's what could put him in prison. Then I realized sadly that it couldn't.

"Was a bigamist," I said. "Isn't one now."

12

NOT OUR PLEADINGS, PROTESTATIONS, OR rain of questions could keep Loretta there five more minutes.

"Dammit—*you're* stunned? How do you think *we* feel finding out the creep killed her? And we just assumed you knew she'd married him."

Our blank faces spoke for us, and Loretta jerked on her coat. "Look, there's nothing else we can tell you and no way we can help. Besides"—she moved to the door—"I can't keep Liza waiting down in that lobby indefinitely. If you can think of anything we can do, give a call. Right now I'm going home to oblivion. Come along, Father."

"I'll be down in five minutes." It was said gently but firmly, and he stayed in his chair.

Loretta shrugged and started out. Sadd said, "I'll go down with you," and they left.

I looked at the priest gratefully but had qualms as to how all this was affecting him. I had no doubt he was a strong and saintly man, but when, at his age, an abyss opens before one . . . I needn't have worried. His hands, unlike Loretta's flailing ones, lay quietly in his lap, and he said, "You see, I always felt so badly because I'd married them. And I'd advised against it."

Henry said, "Did you suspect he was up to something?"

"No, not at all." Father Bob shook his head decidedly. "I just didn't think they were suited. And I sensed he was dragging his feet. But Janet was infatuated and pressing for marriage."

Oh, poor Janet, poor Janet . . .

Dan said, "How long after they were married did he split?"

"Did he what?" The dear man touched his hearing aid distrustfully.

"Leave—take off."

"Oh. Er—a few months, I think. I can't recall exactly. But he must have been planning it for some time because he took everything. It was quite a clean sweep."

He stood up and looked around for his coat. Henry got it from the closet and helped him into it, starting to zip it as Father Bob said, "You asked about that poor girl's child. Yes, it was born, and I baptized it."

Henry stopped zipping, and Dan and Kit were out of their chairs. Dan said, "When?" and Kit said, "Where?"

"Oh, dear, I wish I could be more helpful." Father finished the zipping himself and stood concentrating. "Well, I can answer the 'where.' The little Catholic church in Bryantville. The 'when' I'm hazy on. Let me think . . . We'd all gone out to the closing of St. Elizabeth's Home. It must have been summer because Janet held a big picnic for the children—they were dispersing

106

to other homes—and the girl we're speaking of called me in Hartford where I was stationed"—he began to look pleased as recollection dawned—"and she asked me if I was coming to the picnic." Now he was beaming. "We can almost assume, then, that she worked at the home, can't we? Well, I said I was, and she asked if I would baptize the baby that afternoon. So it must have been a Sunday—in those days baptisms were always on Sunday afternoons"—continued beaming—"and I told her to take the baby to the church and I'd slip away from the picnic. I said nothing to Janet—why distress her?"

Kit and I said together, "Was it a boy or a girl?"

The poor dear's face fell again. "Now that, I don't remember at all."

Oh, blast. "Perhaps you recall the name the child was given." A sad shrug. "The date—do you remember the date?"

He struggled. "It must have been summer—I mentioned that—and a Sunday . . . but you want the year . . ."

Dan said, "That should be easy, Father. What year did St. Elizabeth's Home close?"

Easy? No way. "Some time in the late sixties, I think." We were silent. "I'm not helping much, am I?"

I said, rather desperately, "If we had even an approximate date, we might trace the birth record, assuming the child was born in Bryantville."

"It wasn't." He spoke with sudden assurance. "She told me she'd gone away to a relative somewhere."

There goes the ballgame, I thought.

Then Henry said, while moving around the room, "Do you remember anything at all about that picnic, Father? Who was there? Who might—"

"Mrs. Vaughan!" said Kit. "She might . . ."

Father's bleak smile put an end to that. "At this point Retta's memory is worse than mine. I'm not even sure . . ." Then he stopped and took two steps toward my bed, and I was afraid the poor thing was going to pitch across my knees.

"The picnic! I'm so glad you mentioned that. I have a distinct recollection that everybody there was talking about the assassination of Robert Kennedy. What year was that?"

"June sixth, 1968," said Henry, who had been a youthful admirer. "And I think it was a Thursday, so the following Sunday . . . Would the record of the baptism still be at the church?"

"Oh, yes."

"But you don't remember the name of the mother or the sex of the child?" said Kit.

"I'm afraid not."

I said with both hope and dread, "Was it the only baby baptized that day?"

"No, I seem to recall . . . several others."

Strike three. He looked exhausted and apologetic, and I was ashamed of us. I said, "Father Bob, you've been wonderful, and we won't keep you another minute. Thanks ever so much."

He looked down at his hands, one holding the prayer book and the other the scapular. "Do you want me to have these?"

"Of course."

"Well . . . thank you." He put the prayer book in his pocket. "But I think Janet would have wanted you to have this." He laid the scapular on the table beside me. What could I do but return his thanks and ask Henry to take Father to the elevator?

Dan and Kit and I sat in depressed silence. Then Kit said, "Even if we had everything—right down to the person's phone number—would it necessarily do us any good?"

"No, not necessarily." I reached for the card propped against the poinsettia. "Because first, this person may have no idea who his or her father is, or second, may know but be fond of him and anxious to protect him—"

"—but third," said Dan, "this person may know Papa and hate his guts and be willing to rat."

"One of which," said Kit, "we're supposed to find out—beginning with the zinger of whether the person is living or dead, male or female—all in forty-eight hours."

"Not worth it," I said, taking the card from its little envelope. "Let's drop it." I read the card aloud in a voice that ended in a screech. " 'Take good care of yourself. Dwight.' "

Dan and Kit said some inelegant things, and I tore the card to pieces. "*Worth it?* I take back everything I said—worth it! Even if we make fools of ourselves trying!"

Dan said, "When do we leave for Bryantville?"

"Right now." They leaped up. "But first take this plant to the chapel and may the poor lovely thing not die of shame to think who bought it. Get any scrap of information you can—if we can't use it, maybe Captain Redmond can someday—but be back tomorrow because I have just made a knockout decision!"

Henry and Sadd walked back into the room as I practically shouted the last words. They stopped dead, and Sadd said, "Let me guess: you're going to Pushing Murder on Christmas Eve as *Mrs.* Santa Claus."

"You're darned close."

They looked at me aghast, and I added, "We're *all* going to Pushing Murder on Christmas Eve, and I'm going as Clara Gamadge!"

13

LETDOWN. IMPATIENCE. ANXIETY.

All are inevitable after one has ridden the crest of excitement, endeavor, and expectation. Now comes that dreary stretch of enforced inactivity and suspension. If only life were an old, pat, ninety-minute, black-and-white movie; no waits, months and years telescoped into a dreamy montage, happy ending always promised, always delivered.

I voiced this sentiment to Sadd as he and I sat the next afternoon in the little waiting room at the end of my hall. He was reading—what else?—and I was staring morosely at the Christmas tree. We were the only ones availing ourselves of the festive nook, and I commented that I supposed hospitals sent as many people home for Christmas as possible. Sadd grunted.

I reached for my newly issued walker, hauled myself from the wheelchair, and stumped to the window. The beginning of snow—from one flake to ten million in two minutes.

"It's the blasted waiting," I stumped back to the

111

wheelchair and sank into it. "I wonder if it's snowing in Bryantville."

"Sounds like an old song." Sadd turned a page. "I wonder if it's snowing in Bryantville, dear,/The way it used to at this time of year,/When our love was young—"

"They're probably digging out somewhere around Peekskill, and Dan's cast isn't helping."

"Peekskill is in New York. You go nowhere near it to get to Connecticut."

"It just sounds like the kind of place one might get stranded." My entire attention was fixed on the elevator door.

"Clara"—Sadd closed his book—"what exactly do you expect them to come back with?"

"With the names of the babies who were baptized in—what's the name of that church?"

"St. Camillus, according to the Catholic Directory down in the office."

"So—in St. Camillus Church on Sunday, June ninth, 1968."

"Suppose there were ten or fifteen?"

"Father Folsom said 'several others.' That doesn't sound like ten or fifteen."

"No. In fact, the whole thing sounds much more like the proverbial needle in a haystack."

My face must have told him to quit it, for he opened his book again and said, "Speaking of St. Camillus, he just might be your man. It seems he is a patron of the sick."

"I'm not sick," I said crossly, then looked at the worn

112

volume he held. "Is that the book you took from the chapel library?"

"Yes. Butler's *Lives of the Saints.* Classic devotional work. I was hoping it was an eighteenth-century edition, and I was going to ask the hospital if they'd like me to sell it for them. Unhappily, it's an *updated*—appalling word—edition from 1956. Would you like to hear about St. Camillus?"

"Not especially." I looked longingly down the hall. "Henry and Tina and Hen are coming. They're doing last-minute shopping."

Sadd read: " 'Camillus De Lellis was born in 1550 at Bocchianico. He grew to be a young man of uncertain temper, quarrelsome and addicted to gambling. Camillus was converted to a life of unstinting care of the sick after entering a hospital in Rome with a diseased *leg.'* What did I tell you? Your patron to a T."

"I hardly have a diseased leg."

"Picky, picky, picky."

He was smiling at me, and I felt suddenly ashamed. I said, "Sadd, I'm sorry—I'm lousy company. Here you are trying to cheer me up and being more of a saint than anybody in that book, and here I am being a rotten sport." I held out my hand, and he squeezed it. "Read me some more about St. Camillus and—hey, here's the gang!"

The elevator had discharged Henry, Tina, and Hen, followed, I then saw, by Dr. Cullen. I waved, they saw me, then stood in a conspiratorial little knot.

"You've been informed on," Sadd said.

As they advanced, Henry and Tina avoided my eyes,

but Dr. Cullen fixed me with hers and Hen came and kissed me.

I said, "Doctor, what a terrific suit. Blue is definitely your color. I love—"

"Mrs. Gamadge, it's insane of you to think of going anywhere tomorrow except straight home."

"But look!" I hoisted myself to the walker and took five steps. "And I'm a pro in that wheelchair. In fact, I'll stay in it if you think it would be better."

"I think it would be better to go directly to your son's house. I said you could go *home* tomorrow, not to a crowded little shop where the man who has already tried to kill you—"

"—might try again? Decked out as Santa Claus? Ridiculous."

"Mom," said Henry, "Dunlop has helpful pals, as you very well know."

"And you would be his dream hostage," said Tina, "as you also very well know."

I said grimly, "Hen, run down to Gran's room and get that big box of chocolates."

He ran, and I glared at my son and his wife. "Snitchers!"

Sadd said, "Clara, you're being childish." He stood up. "Excuse me, I must return a book to the library."

It sounded so ludicrous that nobody believed it and everyone laughed at his drolly inventive exit line. Dr. Cullen sat down in Sadd's chair and said patiently, "Mrs. Gamadge, what exactly do you expect to accomplish by this excursion to your friend's store?"

"This!" I had gotten back into the wheelchair, and

now I backed it up and drove it toward them. They automatically started away, and I cried gleefully, "See! I create a diversion! 'I need air' or some such, Santa Dunlop is trapped in a circle of children, one of you grabs Sal—bingo!—she's out of there and safely ours till we can have Dunlop arrested."

I smiled at them triumphantly, but my smile was not returned.

Tina said, "Clara, every one of us, at some point, has paid a visit to Pushing Murder. We've all seen a guy, big, young, goony—our descriptions tally—who's always there, quote 'helping.' He's a quote 'acquaintance' of Mr. Dunlop's, and he's good for carrying stock, et cetera, but not, according to himself, quote 'into books.' "

"More into muggings," said Henry. "So no need to tell you, Mom, that Dunlop is well covered."

I sat fuming, and Hen returned with the box of candy. His father told him to pass it, and everybody declined except Dr. Cullen who politely took a chocolate. Hen sat down with the box on his lap, and Tina said, "Take two," and confiscated it.

"Delicious—a brandied cherry." Dr. Cullen took a tissue from her pocket and wiped her fingers. "I understand your young friends have gone to Connecticut to do some tracking."

I nodded wearily. "Yes. To track a person who may be male or female, who may be living or dead, who may or may not—oh, the heck with it."

She stood up and pulled the walker to me. "Let's see you walk down to your room."

115

I had the uncomfortable feeling that my family was watching my wobbly progress, and that Dr. Cullen was doing this on purpose to reinforce her point. No question, the hall looked unbearably long. I thought of that wonderful scene in *The Barretts of Wimpole Street* in which Charles Laughton, everybody's favorite sadist, challenges the invalid Norma Shearer to ascend the stairs. Well, if Norma could do it, I could, but I wished there was a Fredric March to scoop me up in his arms. I plodded grimly on, Dr. Cullen strolling beside me chatting about her daughter's forthcoming wedding. I asked a few polite questions to show her I had the breath, but my morale was cascading. As we came abreast of the elevator, the door opened and Dan and Kit emerged.

They were smiling, but Kit said, "Now, don't get your hopes up too high."

My morale did a U-turn. "Tell me! Tell me!" I all but trotted to the door of my room, and Dr. Cullen said, "Let me not stand in the path of justice. I'll see you tomorrow, Mrs. Gamadge, and remember—straight home."

As I turned to wave to her, I noticed that Dan and Kit were accompanied by a little boy with very dark hair and a little woman with very orange hair.

Kit said, "This is my Mom, Mrs. Kitenski, and Danny. We were hoping Hen might be here."

"I am!" Hen and his parents had converged on us, and I gaily beckoned everyone into my room as I told Mrs. Kitenski what a great daughter she had.

She said, in a wonderful Brooklyn accent, "Here's the

reason we came. There's this Christmas party in the kids' wing tomorrow—Gail knows all the nurses—they told her—and she thought I could take Danny and—what's your name again, honey?—over there to help decorate the place with the usual junk."

We all said great, terrific, et cetera, and I clumped toward the bed, then stopped, grateful they were all engaged in parental instructions for behavior, because I didn't want them to see what I saw. It was red and flat and lay on my pillow. I grabbed it—a plastic bag with the Pushing Murder logo, something—paper?—crackling inside. I shoved it in the pocket of my robe as Kit and Tina came to help me into bed.

"Don't you want to take your robe off?" asked Tina.

"Not for the moment." I clutched the thing, trying to decide if I should show it at once or first hear about what I mustn't get my hopes up about—what syntax! Sadd would expire. They were all peeling off coats and Henry was opening wine, and there was a general air of anticipation and progress. But the thing was like a live coal in my pocket, and I knew it would prevent me from concentrating. I accepted a glass of wine from Henry and said, "I hate to upstage you guys, but we better see what this is first. It was on my pillow."

I pulled it out, red and crumpled. Dan leaped to his feet and grabbed it. He took out a sheet of paper and read the handwritten scrawl. " 'Dear Clara, You and Sadd are having such a nice visit at the end of the hall that I hate to butt in. Besides—' "

"My God!" I cried. "He had to have walked out of that elevator, and I never had my eyes off it!"

117

"No, there are stairs," said Kit.

" '—besides, I was afraid of tiring you, and nothing must do that. Which reminds me, Clara, don't get in touch again with that boring pair of old-timers up in Fairfield. They might tire you *to death.* Dwight.' "

14

SO SATED WERE WE WITH THE MAN'S VENAL-
ity that everyone was more curious than outraged.

How did he know they had come here?

Henry said, "You told Vaughan and Father Folsom
not to say anything—"

"And I'm positive they didn't," I said.

We agreed on this. Then Sadd said, "Perhaps inadver-
tently? Let's say he calls them as Mr. Anybody making
a charitable appeal for the hospital, and this leads them
to innocently reveal . . ." We were all shaking our
heads. He shrugged. "I rather like my scenario."

Tina stated it flatly. "Somebody had to tell him."

We seemed to realize with one accord that Dan and
Kit hadn't spoken. All eyes focused on them, and I said,
"Do you know who?"

"We can guess," said Kit.

We all jabbered at them to speak! speak! as the door
opened and D.N. appeared with my medicine.

"No more of those things!" I said in exasperation.

"But the doctor hasn't discontinued—"

"I have. I've discontinued as of this moment."

She went out with an "I shall report this" look, and they all began scolding me and saying I was taking matters into my own hands and was this wise, and I said who cared and Dan and Kit should start talking.

Dan began, "Well, it snowed like you've never seen, and Kit had to do most of the driving, of course. It's a good thing we got to Bryantville before it was buried, which was already happening. St. Camillus had to be at the far end of town, but the guy at the gas station said we'd see a bunch of cars because they were practicing the Christmas pageant and his kid was one of the Wise Men. We got there and pulled into the first available snowdrift, and Kit said what a time to ask anybody to look into their files and they probably wouldn't give us the time of day."

"But I was wrong," said Kit. "A big, hefty Sister was directing the show, and when we asked where we could find the pastor, she said across the street, the brick house, and wouldn't we like to stay and watch the rehearsal and her niece was one of the angels. We said we'd love to but we had a long trip back to New York, so we plowed across the street and rang the bell, and this fiftyish priest came to the door and said he was Father Dillon and what could he do for us? Dan showed him our credentials, and he said come on in and would we like some coffee? He warned it would have to be instant because he made lousy coffee and his housekeeper was over at the church watching the rehearsal because her grandson was a shepherd."

Tina giggled. "Are you two trying to drive us crazy with suspense?"

Sadd said, "I love it. Don't skip a single angel or shepherd."

"Well, maybe one or two," I said, my heart beating a bit more quickly.

Dan said, "Well, the coffee was a godsend, and we told him we wanted to check a baptism record, and he said certain ones were confidential and did this have anything to do with an adoption? We said it had to do with tracing somebody in the cause of justice and our middle name was confidentiality. He said the files were in his office, so we went in there and asked him if he remembered St. Elizabeth's Home, and he said no, he'd only been at St. Camillus ten years but he'd heard about St. Elizabeth's and it had been right down the street and it was now a bed and breakfast."

Janet's dream home . . . now a bed and breakfast.

"Now me," said Kit. "He takes this big old registry out of a file and says what year did we want, and we say 1968, and he says whoops—wrong one—this is 1910, when the parish was founded, to 1950—and you think the suspense is killing *you*?—and he takes out another, newer-looking one and puts it on the desk and says what month and day, and we say Sunday, June ninth."

Dan waved his cast. "We wanted to jump up and look over his shoulder, but we sat tight, and he starts flipping pages and finally he says here we are, Sunday, June ninth, four baptisms, looks like one boy and three girls, which one do you want?"

"Well, that did it." Kit was on her feet. "Dan said did he mind if we took a look, and Father Dillon said not

121

at all, and he starts to turn the book around and then takes another look and smiles and says—and I remember this exactly—'Dear old Monsignor Tanner was of the old school—Latin yet.' "

Kit unzipped her fanny pack, took out a piece of paper, and handed it to me. "This is what I wrote down."

Henry and Tina were on either side of the bed, and Sadd said, "There's no room for me. Read it aloud."

I murmured, "No glasses. You, Henry."

He read:

Timothy James, parents Mark and Donna Giordano
Patricia Louise, parents John and Elaine Bluette
Laura Mary, parents Steven and Joan McGovern
Elizabeth Ann, mother Catherine Halcombe,
Patre Ignoto

Sadd said into the silence, "Father unnamed."

"But you know what?" said Dan. "I think the 'Elizabeth' would have done it for us."

Nobody was moving except for Kit, who was not only moving but almost prancing. Dan was grinning alternately at me and at her. He said, "Okay, go ahead and finish it."

Kit said, "We asked Father Dillon if he knew anybody who might remember Catherine Halcombe, and he said his housekeeper might because she'd lived in Bryantville all her life. We went across the street, and now the angels and shepherds were out front of the church having a snowball fight, and Father introduced us to a nice older lady, Mrs. Locke, who said sure she remembered Cathy Halcombe. Cathy used to do her hair years ago—her mother owned the beauty shop in Bryantville—and Cathy was a sweet girl who loved kids. In fact, she used to volunteer at St. Elizabeth's Home, which we'd probably never heard of. There'd been a baby, a girl, as Mrs. Locke recalled, but Cathy wasn't married so she'd gone out of town to have it—in those days girls had the decency to do that, said Mrs. Locke—and then Mrs. Folsom, she was the lady who started St. Elizabeth's, was real good to Cathy and later found her a job over in Bridgeport or Stamford or someplace in that area, and after that Mrs. Locke lost track of her, but she did hear that Cathy had died of cancer a few years ago. As for the daughter, sorry, Mrs. Locke didn't have a clue."

Kit stopped for breath, her cheeks flaming.

I said, "But you do."

"You tell, honey," said Kit. "You did it."

"No, go ahead." Dan looked happy and magnanimous.

"No, you."

"For heaven's sake!" cried Henry. "One of you speak—and no angels and shepherds!"

They laughed joyously, and Dan was on his feet. "All the way back in the car it was bugging me—something Loretta Vaughan said when she was here. We'd just hit the Hutch Parkway when it clicked. Kit pulled into that first gas station, and I made the call. A voice said, 'Mrs. Vaughan's residence, Liza Halcombe speaking.'"

Maybe three seconds, then we broke up. Tina hugged Dan, Kit hugged Henry, they all hugged me, and Sadd

123

said, "Don't *I* get hugged?" Both Tina and Kit descended on him, and he emerged disheveled and crimson with delight.

I gasped, "How much does she know?"

Dan raised his shoulders. "Maybe everything, maybe nothing. But she sure as hell must have been chatting to Dad about how her week went. I didn't dare take it any farther—I was afraid I'd blow it. So I just said sorry, wrong number, and hung up."

15

IT WASN'T UNTIL ABOUT EIGHT O'CLOCK
that night that depression began to set in.

We had a plum, but was it too late to use it?

Mrs. Kitenski had returned with the boys, and I'd
sent everybody out to supper with instructions to go
straight home afterward. No one, I emphasized *no one*,
was to come back to the hospital that night. Next day,
Christmas Eve, they'd all go—if I promised not to—to
Pushing Murder for a few hours in the morning. They'd
keep their eyes peeled (another expression Sadd said he
must find the derivation of), give Santa a hand, chat,
shop, and look for any possibility of spiriting Sal away.
It was a very dim hope, tacitly acknowledged so by
all. We agreed that they'd return to the hospital for a final conference before I was discharged at noon.

Now I lay in the semidarkness wondering if Liza
Halcombe was in league with her father. *Patre Ignoto*.
Who had revealed his identity to her? A forgiving Catherine? A calculating Allen Quinn? And when? Years
ago? Last week? The silent, almost thirty-year gap between that June Sunday in 1968 and Dan's phone call

this afternoon maddened me. "Sorry, wrong number" had been the right move on Dan's part, but where did it leave us? To ask the girl to come see me was as good as inviting her father. I shivered as I thought of her describing to him—innocently or not—her drive to the hospital with "the boring pair of old-timers."

I glanced for solace toward my suitcase. Tina had brought it, and it lay open on a chair, a blessed symbol of my release tomorrow. Was it really less than a week since I went sprawling on the sidewalk in front of Pushing Murder, dimly hearing the siren and wondering, as one always does, what poor wretch the ambulance was speeding to? And was it only a few days since the realization that a pleasant acquaintance was a monster?

The black window was packed with snow, and now it was strains of "Hark! The Herald Angels" that filtered up. I decided to take a turn up and down the room on my walker. Good practice for tomorrow when I still secretly hoped I could cajole my family into . . . I'd give anything to face Dwight Dunlop behind his flowing fake beard and create the scene of my life.

I groped along the bed rail for the control and brought myself to a sitting position. I swung both legs out of the bed and the cast clunked to the floor. Steadying myself with it, I did a toe search with the other foot and found a slipper. Walker just within reach. Yeah—here we go. Ride a cock horse to Banbury Cross,/To see an old lady upon a white horse—read *walker*. Now, what name had been nagging at me? . . . Ah, yes. Captain Redmond.

Could I trust him to be forbearing if I shared the information about Liza Halcombe? I hated to part with my golden nugget if it developed that she was innocent and oblivious, but should Dwight make good his escape the day after tomorrow, and the horrid possibility was fast becoming a horrid probability, then the captain could have anything I had—I'd promised him that. How could I get to the girl obliquely? Through Loretta Vaughan? I cringed at a mental picture of "Retta" staring at me in disbelief, taking another swig, and saying, "My God! Do you mean to tell me that that girl . . . !"

I was cold. No robe for my perambulation. "Hark! The Herald Angels" had dissolved into "Away in a Manger." I crept back to my own manger, got into it, snapped out my reading light, and closed my eyes on the darkness. Presently I knew the door had opened because the light from the hall struck across my eyelids.

A girl's voice said, "Are you asleep, Mrs. Gamadge?"

"No."

"I'm sorry it's so late, but they did say visiting hours are till nine. I'm Liza Halcombe, Mrs. Vaughan's secretary."

I was proud of my calm voice. "The light switch is right there by the door, Liza."

"I won't stay long. I'm sure you're tired." Even in the harsh, overhead glare she was delightful-looking, with brown hair, big eyes, a green, suede coat reaching to boot tops. But I felt it was imperative that I either breathe naturally again or take certain precautionary measures like yelling for help.

I said, "Are you alone?"

"Yes, I am."

Relief, but not total. "Does anyone know you're here?"

"No. Why?"

"Oh, I'm just one of those old folks who worries about young people being out alone in New York at night. Sit down, Liza. I'm so glad you came. I know Mrs. Vaughan thinks the world of you. No, I'm not a bit tired. I guess I'm too happy. I'm going home tomorrow."

"Oh, that's great. For Christmas. Did you have an operation?" She sat, pretty and relaxed in the plastic chair.

"No, an accident. I broke my ankle."

"Oh." She looked away a little. "Actually, I've come to ask your advice about something ... somebody. Mrs. Vaughan said you and your husband used to help people with problems and you still do."

If she says it, I thought, I'm going to need the brandy in that closet. She said it. "It's—it's my father. I'm afraid he has a problem, maybe a serious one."

I have never had hysterics in my life—the real thing, that is, with all the trimmings—and for an instant I thought my time had come. Only compassion for this girl and the thought of the brandy enabled me to say—I hope calmly—"Liza, I'm sure that working for Mrs. Vaughan has given you a horror of alcohol"—she shuddered—"but sometimes older people like myself do need a stimulant."

"Oh, please don't think—"

"So would you mind—there's brandy on that closet

shelf. The doctor said I should take an occasional medicinal sip."

"Yes, of course." She stood up. "Is this plastic glass okay?"

"Fine."

"Maybe I should come back."

"Oh, mercy, no."

She handed me the bottle. Now, it's one thing to be offered a glass; it's another to be handed a bottle. I felt like an old toper as I poured less than I wanted and put the bottle on the table lest I contaminate her further by handing it back. I said, "I certainly want to hear about your father, but first I'd like to know about you. How long have you been working for Mrs. Vaughan?"

"Since my mother died two years ago. She had cancer. I was living with her at the time . . ."

Liza talked on about those last sad days, and I nodded and sipped. I had the sensation of being seated before a jigsaw puzzle, sorting pieces of blue sky, green trees, and pink flowers, and now suddenly discovering a chunk with a face on it.

". . . and Mrs. Folsom was always so good to us. She found Mom that job in Bridgeport and paid for my tuition at business school. But she never knew that Dad came to see us. She told Mom she shouldn't see him again ever. She felt that since my parents were never married—are you sure I'm not tiring you?"

"I'm sure." It's difficult to sip brandy while holding one's breath, but I managed. "How often did your dad come see you?"

"Not very often." Liza crossed one chic boot over the

other. "Sometimes it would be years. He's one of those guys who just can't seem to settle down. And I know he's had some run-ins with the law and he's quite a womanizer. Mom and I had no illusions. We knew all his faults."

All, poor child? Not quite all.

"And she used to give him money, and that kind of made me sore. But she really loved him, and I guess I do too. If you knew him, you'd understand. He's very charismatic."

The derivation of the word flashed on me, and it was my turn to shudder.

Liza went on. "I felt really guilty when Mrs. Folsom recommended me for the job with Mrs. Vaughan. She said not to tell her who I was because one of Dad's escapades had to do with a children's home Mrs. Folsom started and Mrs. Vaughan might remember him. Mom worked at the home, so I guess I was part of that escapade." She smiled. "It was called St. Elizabeth's, and that's how I got my name. But I grew up adoring Liza Minnelli, so I made it that."

I began to feel sad. Very sad.

Now Liza leaned forward earnestly. "I haven't seen Dad since Mrs. Folsom's terrible murder, but I've talked to him on the phone and he seems upset. I have this awful feeling he may be connected with it somehow. On the other hand"—her face brightened, and I thought how quickly love welcomes hope—"it could be because he's splitting up with his current lady friend." She stopped and looked down at her boots. Just "lady friend," eh? Typical Dwight deception; much less heinous breaking up with one of those. Liza looked back at me. "I'm not exactly sure where they live, but I think it's in this area because he said he'd like to come to my place for Christmas. He'll be there tomorrow afternoon, he said."

I began to feel glad. Very, very glad.

"Where do you live, Liza?"

"Two seventy-four West End Avenue. I could never afford it except Mrs. Vaughan helps with the rent. I wanted to put her name on the buzzer with mine, but she wouldn't let me. She's been great. She gave me a nice big check and told me to take all Christmas week off. I could buy Dad a present, but he'd probably rather have the money. No, on second thought"—this happy chatter was unbearable—"he sounded rather flush. You know what he said? He'd like to take me on a cruise over New Year's."

I began to feel mad. Very mad.

"So maybe there isn't a problem, Mrs. Gamadge, and I'm just imagining things."

"No, Liza, you aren't."

I put my glass down in order to look away from her startled face.

"What do you mean?"

A brisk voice from the door said, "Visiting hours are over in ten minutes." Liza stood up uncertainly. I put out my hand, and she took it, and I drew her to the bed. I said, "Sit down here, dear. I never keep hospital rules. They'll be happy to throw me out of here tomorrow."

She was on the edge of the bed, her eyes wide and frightened. "Please—tell me."

131

"Tell *me* something first. You must have mentioned to your father that you drove Mrs. Vaughan and Father Folsom here to the hospital."

Bewilderment. "Sure. I was telling him what I'd been doing. He always asks. What's that got to do with anything?"

"And you're sure he doesn't know you're here now?"

Annoyance. "No—I told you. Look, Mrs. Gamadge, if you're going to keep asking me all this stuff and not tell me—"

"I'm through asking, Liza. And I'm sorry. It's just very difficult for me to tell you . . ." I ground to a halt in anguish.

Anger. "Tell me what, for God's sake?"

I couldn't say it. I *could not* say it. I could not send this girl out into the night alone with the knowledge that her father . . . And now I proceeded to make it worse. I said, "Promise me something. Promise you won't tell your father you've seen me."

"Don't worry." The bright young voice had gone shrill. She walked to the door. "You know what I think? I think you're a big fake. You see yourself as a red-hot problem solver, and all you are is an old lady who drinks brandy and has delusions of—of—grandeur. Keep going, Mrs. Gamadge, and you'll be right out there with Loretta Vaughan in la-la land."

"Liza—wait!" Could I recoup? "I want—that is—I have a confession to make."

She leaned against the wall by the door in a martyr's stance. Lord help me, this had to be good, the kind of "confession" she'd understand. I started slowly and humbly, groping . . .

"You're right—I guess I am kind of crazy-sounding, but not because of the brandy. Because of something—er—else that I hope you won't think is crazy and maybe you'll understand." I had it! "It's because of your father's lady friend. I know her."

16

LIZA PUSHED HERSELF AWAY FROM THE WALL and walked back to the bed. She said, "Then you must know Dad too."

"I've met him. You're right—he's very attractive. My friend is distraught because she doesn't want to break off with him."

Liza frowned. "You mean he's walking out?"

"Yes."

"Figures." Her frown deepened.

"That's why I didn't want you to tell him you'd seen me." This has to be exactly right, Clara. "It might make him"—I got out the preposterous word—"uncomfortable. . . . And I feel awful for her."

To my enormous relief, she nodded sympathetically. Thank God she was young and love was all.

"You're very considerate." She touched my hand. "I'm sorry if I—"

"Please, not another word; I was handling it badly." I was also breathing again.

Liza pulled a green wool cap from her pocket. "I'm

not going to ask who she is or where they are. I just feel real, real sorry for her."

"So do I."

"Is she young?"

"No. My age."

"Oh, damn. The poor thing." She touched my hand again. "Well, I'll say good night. Have a nice Christmas, and I hope I'll see you again sometime."

So do I, Liza, if the time ever comes when you don't hate me too much. She went out with a little wave, and I found a pencil and wrote "274 West End" on the pad, then burst into tears, burying my face in the pillow to drown the sound of my grief. Even the good, gut feeling of success was curdled by my pity for this winning girl, and I wept as I thought of her going home to a rendezvous with shock and horror.

I pulled myself together and reached for the phone. I asked for an outside line, then for the police precinct, then for Captain Redmond. He wasn't there. I gave my name. Would he return the call as soon as possible? He'd know that it was important.

Then I lay staring at the wall. Cancel the conspiratorial gathering at Pushing Murder tomorrow. Just a vigilant presence in the vicinity to watch for Dwight's departure, then the dreadful enlightenment of Sal. She should be taken straight to Henry's. Please God, I'd be there myself by then. Next we would call her son, whom we had purposely left out of the proceedings for fear of too many cooks. Liza would also have to be rescued. Again, Nice Ugly seemed the best place. And Paula was arriving there with her family! And it was

135

Christmas Eve! Two sets of parents, three revved-up kids, a pair of desolate, possibly prostrate guests, Sadd, the original Mr. Bah Humbug, and gimpy me. Tina would never speak to me again. I'd have to give her a really special present. Maybe a pretty suede coat ... the kind Liza was wearing ...

I must have slept in spite of my mental turmoil. A gentle but persistent voice kept saying my name. It sounded like Captain Redmond's, but I hadn't heard the phone ring. I opened my eyes, and he was dimly discernible standing by the bed. He was saying did I realize it wasn't easy to get to see a patient in the middle of the night and he hoped it was worth it. I said I did too and snapped on my reading light to discover Dan on the other side. I said, "Dan, I thought I told—"

"You were overruled. We agreed among ourselves that I'd stand by tonight. Who was the girl?"

"Liza Halcombe."

"I had a hunch."

"Dan," I found myself gulping, "she doesn't know a thing, and she's handing him to us on a silver platter."

"Yes, you were crying your eyes out, so I figured that. Then I heard you call the captain. I was pretty sure he'd come."

"So he came," said that gentleman impatiently. "So let's hear it."

I drew a breath and reached for the pad. Feeble rays of light struggled through the window. It must be warmer. The snow was gone. I said, "Some time after noon today Janet Folsom's killer will walk into 274 West End Avenue. He's a big man in his sixties with blondish white hair, and he goes by the name Dwight Dunlop. He'll be carrying a lot of cash that he's just stolen and he'll—"

"Can you produce the person he's stolen it from?"

"I sure can. What precinct will they take him to?"

"West End Ave., you say? That would be the Twentieth Precinct."

"Dan will bring her there. But Captain"—I sat up and seized his arm—"he *must not get past the street door of that building*. He'll be looking for the name Halcombe, and he mustn't touch that buzzer. Can I trust you for that? He must *not*—"

"Okay, okay. Who's Halcombe?"

"His daughter. She's expecting him, and the poor kid doesn't know a thing. Captain, do I have your solemn promise—"

"Solemn." He pushed me gently back on the pillow. "Do you have any evidence that he did the murder as well as the theft?"

"No, but he has a record going back thirty years, he was a bigamist, his credentials are all fake—"

"Doesn't mean a thing."

"Captain"—I knew I was shrill and irrational—"this man tried to kill me, did kill Janet Folsom, hired somebody to mug Dan—"

"We still have to prove all that, Mrs. Gamadge," said Dan. "The police can only prove the theft."

"Correct," said the captain.

"It may be correct, but it ain't *right*," I muttered.

"Okay." I looked from one to the other in the now almost light room. "How long can you hold him for the theft?"

"Will it be a thousand dollars or more?"

"Much more. And possibly jewelry and—"

"Then that's grand larceny, and we can hold him for five or six days."

"Good." I lay back exhausted, my ankle throbbing. "I'll get the evidence you need by then. I don't know how, but I'll get it. I promised you the killer for Christmas, Captain, and isn't this Christmas Eve?" The way I felt, it could have been the Fourth of July.

"It sure is, and you've done a great job." He took my hand. "I'll have that address covered right now. He may show up sooner than you think."

"I doubt it. He won't have all the cash he wants till the store closes at noon." I glanced at the captain quickly. Had I said too much? Had I ever mentioned Pushing Murder to him? Blast my poor befuddled head. I waited for him to say "What store?" but he was looking at me thoughtfully.

"You've been protecting somebody," he said. "Is this the person he's ripping off?"

"Yes."

"His wife?"

"Yes."

He continued to study me. "You seem big on protecting people, Mrs. Gamadge. Is there anyone else he might get to if we miss him at his daughter's?"

I sat up again fast. If they miss him. We'd have Sal out, but were there two possible understudies waiting in the wings? I looked at Dan, and he said, "Those relatives of Janet Folsom's in Fairfield, Mrs. Vaughan and the priest."

The captain looked surprised. "Dunlop knows them?"

"He sure does," said Dan.

"Knows where they live?"

"Yup. And knows that they know what we know."

"Can they be put on ice till we have him?"

"You bet they can!" I reached for the phone as it rang.

Dr. Cullen's voice said severely, "Mrs. Gamadge, I've just been talking to your son."

"At this hour? I'm a little surprised that you'd call—"

"He called me."

"Then he ought to be ashamed of himself."

"He said you'd be awake and—his word—'perking.'" Very severe now. "He knows, as I do, that you need rest if you're going home today, and you refused your medication. I've just called the hospital, and you're to get a shot. If you refuse it, I won't discharge you."

Click. Damn. I said, "Guys, they're going to sic a nurse on me with a needle."

"Good idea," said the captain. He walked to the door, smiled back at me, and went out, passing Sister Agnes.

I said, "Dan—quick—do you have Loretta Vaughan's number?" He produced his notebook. "Get her, and listen on the extension. Can you hold off one minute, Sister?"

139

"Not one minute—the way Dr. Cullen sounded." Whammo! "And you might as well go back to your post, Mr. Schenck. She won't be talking to you for very long."

Sister trotted out, and I commenced a determined effort to combat the stuff. "Dan, Loretta doesn't know who Liza is. Janet got her the job and insisted—"

He handed me the receiver, and Loretta's surprisingly unsleepy voice said hello.

"Loretta, this is Clara Gamadge. Awful hour to call you."

"What's up?"

"I want you and Father Bob out of your house. We're closing in on you-know-who, and there's no telling—"

"You mean you've actually got the bastard?"

"No, but please God, today. If there's a slip, he might head for your place."

"Good. I'll shoot him."

"Loretta, be serious. Think of Father Bob."

"Oh, he's gone."

"Gone where?"

"To the monastery in Hazelton, New York. He goes there every Christmas."

"Thank goodness. Then you're alone?"

"Yes. I gave Liza the week off."

Liza. The name penetrated the haze that was beginning, ever so insidiously, to roll in. I said rapidly, "Here's what I want you to do: take the next train to New York, then a cab to my son's house in Brooklyn

Heights." What was I *doing*? Adding yet another be-draggled soul to that menage? "His address is—"

"Nonsense. I wouldn't dream of imposing. If you really think I should get out of here, I'll go to a hotel."

"Good." I fought bravely. "I'm going home—that is, to Henry's." I thought of her alone in a hotel on Christmas. "Come see us tomorrow."

"You wouldn't want me. I'll be stoned all day."

"You can be stoned there." My own stoning was happening fast now.

"Well, I might—hey! I have a great idea! Forget a hotel—I'll go to Liza's."

Mother of God, had she really said that?

"She's always after me to come and see the place. I'll call her right now."

"Loretta"—I got the words out—"don't go to Liza's."

"Why not?"

I looked wildly at Dan as I shot over the falls.

Sal's face, wet and haggard, was bending over mine. Henry had her by the shoulders.

"Oh, Clara, Clara, Clara!"

"Sal, honey, I'm so sorry, so sorry." I looked up at Henry. "When?"

"About an hour ago. Just before noon." Henry pulled her gently up and eased her into a chair, which she hitched toward the bed, weeping convulsively. "Dan and I were across the street in a coffee shop. He came out with a suitcase. I went in to Sal, and Dan trailed him in a cab. He walked about five blocks and went

141

into a car rental place. But when he came out, he didn't
head uptown toward West End. He headed south. Dan
got the license plate, but he lost him at the Holland
Tunnel."

17

CRUSHING DISAPPOINTMENT DID A JOB ON MY
priorities. I should have been thinking of poor Sal as
she sat crumpled by the bed, or of the anxiously waiting
Liza. Instead, I was engulfed by rage and mortification.

Who had tipped him off—*who*?

I thought of the fruitless police watch at West End
Avenue and ground my teeth. Henry brought me to my
senses. Taking Sal's hand, he said, "Come on, Sal,
you're going to our place."

But she only leaned forward and put her head on my
bed. I was afraid she was on the point of collapse. I
said, "Sal, honey, please go home with Henry. I'll be
there myself very shortly." Another grievance washed
over me. "Why aren't I *out of here*?" I threw back the
covers. "Henry, get my clothes from that closet before
I go stark, staring mad!"

"Take it easy, Mom. There's procedure. You're not
discharged till four o'clock."

"Four! I was told noon!"

"But you slept through, so Dr. Cullen pushed it up.
She wants to be sure you're—"

"What time is it now?" I asked wildly as a nurse came in with a lunch tray. The sight of it made me sick.

"It's about two, Mrs. Gamadge. You missed lunch." She looked at my distraught visitor and almost shrugged; everybody was used to it—this room was a nuthouse. She deposited the tray and went out.

"Henry, I'll never forgive you for calling Dr. Cullen. I'd be out of here now if you hadn't—is that soup? Make Sal take some."

But she shook her head violently without raising it. I said despairingly, "Why on earth didn't you take her straight home?"

"Because I told him I wanted to see you first." Muffled voice from beneath the bowed head. Then it came up. "I had to tell you how sorry I am for causing you all this grief, Clara."

"Don't be an idiot. Just let Henry—"

"Yes, I'll go." She rose shakily. "But only if Henry promises to let me crawl in a corner of his attic or somewhere so I won't spoil Christmas for everybody. But first I have to call Larry in Baltimore—"

"Your son's in Baltimore?" I said.

She nodded. "With his wife's family."

Henry said, "Now, that *would* be spoiling a Christmas for somebody." He put his arm around her. "Ours is going to be just fine, and you're going to be part of it, so let your son enjoy his and call him Sunday."

Greatly relieved, I took her hand. "Darling Sal, I know it's a platitude, but this too shall pass. You'll get over it and be happy again, you will, you will. Just tell me one thing, then beat it. How much did he get?"

Her eyes closed, and she swayed a little. "I'm not sure. A few thousand, maybe. We hadn't banked in a couple of days. He said we should keep—"

"Had you signed anything over to him?" Henry pulled her coat closed.

"No." She swallowed. "After Christmas I planned . . . it was going to be a Christmas present. . . ." She gagged.

"Good!" I said briskly. "Now go. See you in just a couple of hours."

"Bathroom first." She went unsteadily into it.

Gratefully, I seized the moment. "Henry, does she know he killed Janet?"

He looked blank. "No. I mean—how would she?"

I groaned. "This blow is 'Merry Christmas,' that blow will be 'Happy New Year.' "

"By the way, Dan filled us in on what happened last night."

I quaked. "What did he do about Loretta?"

"He told her to go to a hotel. He also told her who Liza is, and he told her to come over to Nice Ugly tomorrow. Good thing it has rubber walls."

"Henry, how can I ever—"

"It's like old times, actually. Remember when Dad would bring in forlorn creatures he was protecting?" I nodded mutely. "Paula's arrived, and she's baking up a storm. Sadd and Dan will be here at four to escort you home. Hope you don't mind a cab."

"A dog cart would be heaven."

"Meanwhile, Dan is standing by to deliver Sal if we get lucky and Dunlop is picked up. And Tina wants to know if she should go up to West End Ave. and fetch Liza."

Oh, Lord, oh, Lord. I rolled over miserably. "How can we? She doesn't know ... I have a wild hope he may show up there yet. You know, he might have taken a circuitous route for safety's sake, mightn't he?"

I looked imploringly at my son, and he nodded. "Sure he might. For safety's sake or"—he zipped his parka—"for whatever reason. By the way, Sadd's on his way here now. You shouldn't be alone."

I stared at him. "Why would that creep Dunlop come here? He's scot-free, dammit."

Henry leaned down and kissed me. "All I know is I won't rest till you're ensconced at Nice Ugly with all the other displaced persons."

Sal came out of the bathroom. I blew her a kiss, she waved wanly, and they left.

I looked at my watch. Two-thirty. I swung my legs out of the bed and pulled on my robe. So help me, I'd be dressed and sitting on my suitcase at the door the way we were at boarding school when it was time to go home for vacation. A very young aide came in and looked at my tray.

"You haven't eaten a thing."

"No." I reached for the walker. "I'm on a hunger strike till I get out of here."

She looked shocked, and I realized the remark was smart-alecky. I smiled. "I'm not hungry. And I'm leaving shortly. I'm saving myself for my daughter's strudel."

146

I kept smiling, and she picked up the tray and said, "Well, Merry Christmas if I don't see you again."

"Same to you, dear."

She left, and I hobbled to the closet. Another boarding school memory swept over me. You wore the uniform for weeks and months, "home clothes" being stored away in a central closet, and now it was time for them again and you hurried there and got out your pretty dress, your pretty coat, and yes, your pretty hat—I smiled at that thought—and you dressed eagerly and paraded a bit. . . .

Almost as eagerly, I took from the closet what Tina had brought. Underwear, plaid skirt, and what was this? A lovely, brand-new turtleneck sweater! But it looked too small. Then again, maybe not—everybody said I'd lost weight. It just might . . . I was positively giggling as I took out the dressy white coat I'd worn to the party at Pushing Murder. I threw it over my arm, and it spread open, displaying an ugly tear and stain from my fall.

I was back on that sidewalk in front of the store, hearing the siren.

The phone rang. Slightly disoriented, I got to it.

"This is Liza, Mrs. Gamadge, and I'm so scared. Dad hasn't come, and this awful guy was just here."

Why was I cold? Because I'd discarded my robe in my eagerness to dress. I said, "What awful guy?" and crawled back into bed.

"He was just a kid—maybe eighteen or twenty—but he was a real punk and he said Dad owed him money for hanging around your floor of the hospital last night.

And then he said Dad still owed him for another job and had told him to come here today and he'd pay him." She was gasping. "And the other job—the other job—"

"Try to keep calm, dear." Oh, how I hated that man. "The other job?"

"He said he'd stolen something for Dad, and I said I didn't believe it, so he showed it to me. It was a letter addressed to you. Oh, Mrs. Gamadge, what's it all about?"

My head was spinning. "It's about murder, you poor, poor kid."

"Oh, God, oh, God. Did you know all this last night?"

"Yes, but I was hoping it wouldn't touch you—yet. Take heart, Liza." I was running out of phrases of consolation. "You'll have lots of love and support. Did this guy by any chance"—but I knew the answer—"give you the letter?"

"No, I didn't have nearly enough money. He said Dad had given him three hundred dollars and owed him another three hundred plus fifty for last night. He said he'd be back in an hour and Dad better be here or he'd take the letter to you. I won't let him in when he comes back, but oh, Mrs. Gamadge—"

Oh, Mrs. Gamadge, you lucky woman. Of course Dunlop had to have that letter. It was his fatal connection with the murdered woman, the statement of his bigamous marriage to her. It would become the driving force in our pursuit of him that he knew we would never abandon.

148

Liza was still "Oh, Mrs. Gamadging," but I broke in, "Liza, I want that letter, and of course you won't let him in when he gets back because you won't be there. In less than an hour my daughter-in-law, Tina, will pick you up and she'll—"

"Oh, but I can't—"

"You can and you must. But I want you to write something now. Get a pencil and paper and an envelope."

"Okay." It was a pathetic whisper, and I seethed as I waited. "What shall I write?"

I dictated slowly: " 'I am waiting for you at the hospital . . . with more money than you were promised . . . I am leaving today . . . I am not going to the address on that letter . . . so if you want the money . . . hurry.' Underline *hurry*."

A pause as she scratched. "Really? You're not going home?"

"No, I'm going to my son's in Brooklyn, where you're going, and we'll have Christmas together." A sob that tore my heart. "On the envelope write 'From Clara Gamadge' and tape it over your buzzer. Then throw something in a bag and wait for Tina. Good-bye for now, Liza—and courage."

I hung up and started to punch Henry's number with shaking fingers. I had a feeling that our mugger would sense Dunlop was a deadbeat and wouldn't waste time on a second visit to West End Avenue. Quite possibly he was on his way to St. Victor's this minute! Then, with a combination of elation and shock, I realized that, because he had failed to make the rendezvous, the same

149

progression of events would undoubtedly occur to Dunlop. My words to Henry, "Why would that creep Dunlop come here?" rang hollowly. He wanted the letter, and I wanted him to want it, but might some appalling twist of fate cause his path to cross Mugger's before my very door?

The phone was saying something about hanging up and trying again. I concentrated and punched.

"Merry Christmas, this is Jane Fortina."

"Janey, get your mother for me quick!"

"Is this you, Gran? Mommy said that would be a nice way to answer the phone today."

"Get your mother, Janey, or Aunt Tina!"

Another receiver was picked up, and my daughter's indignant voice said, "Mom! You never told me all this was going on! Are you okay?"

"Paula, tell Tina to go to the address Dan gave her and get Liza Halcombe—tell her to leave this minute."

"Will do."

"I love you, darling. See you soon." What a family I had!

Now, money. Christmas Eve, after three o'clock—wouldn't you know. One more phone call. Dan answered instantly.

"Dan, I need you right away."

"I was just leaving. Anything wrong?"

"No. Is your bank near you?"

"Branch right down the street."

"Does it have an automatic teller?"

"Yes."

"Will you lend me five hundred dollars and bring it

150

here in a hurry? You'll kill me when I tell you who it's for."

"On my way."

I sat on the edge of the bed and agonized. Suppose Mugger didn't show up before four o'clock. Having agitated for days to leave the place, how could I reasonably delay? Exhaustion, palpitations, a fainting fit? I looked around at the total disarray of the room—enough to make anyone faint. Mustn't pack, mustn't dress. Stay in bathrobe. Lie down and look wan. Wonder aloud if, after all, I really do feel strong enough to—

The phone rang.

"Is this Mrs. . . . ?" He pronounced it something like "garbage" and I knew my prince had come.

18

"YES—YES—THIS IS MRS. GAMADGE. I BE-
lieve you have something to sell me."

"Yeah."

"Good. I'm anxious to buy. Where are you?"

"No dice. How do I know you won't—"

"My dear child, believe me I won't. I only ask because it will take about thirty or forty minutes to get the
cash. Can you be here that soon?"

"Yeah."

"Will five hundred dollars be satisfactory?"

"Yeah!"

"Then bring the letter as quickly as possible. You
know my room number. You were here last night,
weren't you?"

"Yeah."

"If you get here before the cash does, we can chat
while we wait."

"Yeah?"

"Yeah." A blank pause. "Perhaps we can discuss a
career change for you." Clara, don't be cute. "Believe
me, I have absolutely no interest in detaining you, and

I'll be out of here very shortly, so hurry." I became aware of a sort of dim roar in the background. "Can you hear what I'm saying?"

"Yeah."

"What's that noise? Are you in a subway station?"

"I'm downstairs in the hospital lobby. The place is mobbed. Santa Claus just came in."

My heart stopped. Santa Claus. I told myself there *was* a children's party here today and probably a thousand Santas operating in Manhattan at this moment. But if—but if—and if—had he seen Mugger? From the level of noise, I judged the phone to be in an open row of slots, not in a booth. I envisioned the boy standing in full view, turned toward Santa.

I said, "Do what I tell you. Go stand at the main door of the lobby. In just a few minutes a dark-haired man with a mustache will come in. His wrist is in a cast, which you put there."

"Huh?"

"He's the man you took the letter from in the parking garage."

"Yeah? I broke his wrist?" Definite note of pride.

"He won't know you, of course, so say to him, 'Mrs. Gamadge said I should give you the letter and you give me the money.' " I couldn't add the insane words "And don't let Santa see you do it," so I settled for "Maybe you better wait outside. You might miss him in the crowd. Is Santa Claus still there?"

"Yeah. I hope this guy ain't long. It's starting to snow again. Hey—wait."

"What?"

"How do I know you won't have me picked up?"

"What for? You could have just found the letter and be kindly returning it to me. Don't be dumb. Dumb crooks go nowhere."

I hung up, mad with impatience. Sure enough, the window was white again. Traffic would be at a crawl. Oh, Dan, get out of the cab and *run.* I started to pull my clothes on, at the same time moving around the room pitching stuff into the wastebasket or my suitcase. As I tipped the contents of the bedside table drawer, something caught on my fingers—the string of Janet's scapular. I stood staring at it, then I wrapped the string around the two little squares and laid it beside my pocketbook. An amulet. I'd hold it in my hand till I was clear of the hospital. See me safely out, Janet.

Dr. Cullen and a beaming Sister Agnes walked in. I had a feeling they were both immensely relieved to see me go.

"Merry Christmas, Mrs. Gamadge, you're a free woman." The doctor held out her hand smiling, then took my wrist. I hoped my pulse wasn't pounding. "How do you feel?"

"Just great."

"Let me see you move without the walker."

I limped about a little, and she talked about how I should rent one of the things but not rely on it too much, how I was to . . . Dan should be coming through the door just about now, just about now . . . and she would see me at her office in two weeks.

I said, "Thanks for everything, Doctor. Thanks so much."

"I hope all the grief and trouble will be over soon."

"I hope so, too. Thanks again."

She went out, and Sister said, "Who's taking you home?"

"Mr. Saddlier and Dan Schenck. They should be here any minute."

"Here's your instruction sheet and a prescription for medication if you need it." I stuffed them into my pocketbook. "Dr. Cullen will want to see you in two weeks, and Dr. Purdy in four."

"Who?"

"Dr. Purdy. The orthopedist." Was that the name of the ridiculously young man I'd seen twice? "You're going to your son's home in Brooklyn, I understand."

"Yes, I am."

"Well, I guess that's everything. You'll go down in a wheelchair, of course."

"Must I?"

"Oh, yes. You'll be wheeled right to the car. I'll be back when you're ready to go. Anything else I can do for you?"

"Not a thing. You've been wonderful, Sister. I'm very grateful." I added lamely, "I hope I haven't upset things too much."

"Of course not." She patted my hand. "You were fine. You were—well, as one of the nurses said—you were *different*."

She went out, and I smiled to myself. *Different*. A pleasant euphemism for *weird*. Now, if only my two escorts would show up.... I went to the window and looked despairingly out at the thickening white veil. A tap on the door made me turn.

Santa Claus stood there.

I was speechless and motionless as he started to ho-ho-ho cornily. With an effort, I reminded myself that I was not lying helpless in the bed but was at least ambulatory. I said, as steadily as I could, "Thanks for dropping in, Santa. You look real good."

He said, "*Real* is colloquial. *Very* is preferred."

"Sadd! You wretch!" I grabbed a pillow from the bed and hurled it at him, then burst out laughing with relief. "How could you terrify me like that?"

"Sorry. I didn't think I'd fool you." He pulled down his beard and stood comical and contrite, one cotton eyebrow askew. To think it was only dear Sadd, and me envisioning a disguised Dunlop descending on me and Mugger!

I picked up the pillow. "What are you doing in that rig—you, of all people."

"I'm doing the hospital a favor, that's what I'm doing." He pulled off his pom-pommed cap and grinned. "Did you think I was a certain other Santa of our acquaintance? But he's huge. I thought you'd recognize my foreshortened form."

"You nearly foreshortened my life." I stuck his eyebrow back up. "What brought you to this pass?"

"It seems their regular man, one of the hospital custodians, called in sick at the last minute, so they dug out the costume and waylaid the first sucker to park near the cafeteria door. I told them I was about as suited to the role as Herod, but they dragged me in anyway.

156

Lord, this outfit is hot." He tugged at his throat. "The hospital is overheated as it is, and I'm a walking sauna." He put his cap back on with a groan. "Well, I'd better get it over with."

I stopped in the act of adjusting his padding. "You mean you haven't done your stint yet?"

"No. I just came up to tell you I can't go home with you. Will Dan be sufficient escort?"

"Of course." My mouth was a little dry. "Er . . . were you in the lobby just now?"

"The lobby? God forbid. I sneaked up the back stairs. No, my contract calls for one hour in the cafeteria, no more, no less. Well, see you at Nice Ugly tonight. And I'll bet it will never look nicer or less ugly to you."

I nodded, trying to smile. He went out with a wave, and I waved back, my arm feeling stiff. I stood staring into the hall. Berobed patients passed as usual. Nurses passed as usual. One or two, noting my attire, said, "Going home?" "Merry Christmas," "Take care of yourself," and the like.

The phone rang. When I got to it, Dan's voice was low and his words rapid. "Be at your door with your gear. Stand there and wait for me. Don't be alone. Grab somebody to talk to."

"They say I have to go down in a wheelchair."

"Then get in it. I'll be—wait!" Silence. Or rather, he stopped talking; there was the same dim roar I'd heard before. I envisioned a dangling receiver.

"Dan? Dan?" Oh, God, what had happened to him? I

157

shouted into the phone, "Hello! Hello! Can anyone hear me? Dan! *Dan!*"

His breathless voice said, "I'll be right up. I have the letter, but he's killed the kid."

19

MY FIRST THOUGHT WAS THAT I'D BE GRATE-
ful for the wheelchair; I doubted my legs would carry
me even to the door. But I made them take me to where
my coat and bag lay, then to the bedside table for my
pocketbook, and—what was this object?—of course, the
scapular. I picked it up and closed my fist over it. Normal circumstances would then call for a final check of
closet and bathroom, but now normal called for walking
trancelike to the door.

D.N. was passing. She asked happily, "Ready to go,
Mrs. Gamadge?"

"Yes."

"Sister said to let her know. She wants to go down
with you. I'll get a chair."

I stood leaning against the door. An elderly woman
with a cane was approaching. *Don't be alone. Grab
someone to talk to.* I said, "What a pretty robe. It's just
the kind I've been looking for. Where did you get it?"

"My granddaughter gave it to me for Christmas, and
I wouldn't know where she got it, dear. Going home?
Aren't you lucky."

"Yes, I certainly am. How about you?"

"Not for a while, I guess. The doctor told me ..." She was launched on what promised to be complications enough to last till my chair appeared. In fact, it might be wise to hang on to her right to the elevator—safety in numbers.

"... after my hip replacement but before the pin in my knee ..."

Sister Agnes appeared with my chair. She smiled at my companion and said, "Don't stay up too long, Mrs. Potter."

Mind your own business, Sister. "But her case is so interesting." I got into the chair, piling my gear in my lap. "And I've never known a great deal about hip replacements. Do go on, Mrs. Potter."

Sister said, "Where are Mr. Saddlier and Mr. Schenck?"

"Just Mr. Schenck—he's on his way up."

"... but the cartilage was so torn that the pin ..."

The elevator door opened, and Dan ejected like a bullet. In three steps he was beside us seizing the handle of my chair from Sister.

"Not this elevator, Sister. The lobby's a madhouse. There's been an accident, and the police are there. Can we use the service elevator?"

"An accident!" Sister looked horrified. "Of course—down that way—the second left—all the way to the end."

Dan spun me around, and Mrs. Potter and her replacements and pins were a blur. We sped down the hall, Sister hurrying beside us saying something about the service elevator being unheated and I was to put my coat on and she'd get hers and be right with us. She veered off, and Dan dumped my coat unceremoniously over my shoulders and said, "Here's what happened. This big, oafy kid came up to me and said what you'd told him to say, and we swapped the cash for the letter—I checked it first to be sure it was the real McCoy—and he started off and then turned around and said, 'I need the can' and went back into the lobby. Santa was there, but I never suspected a thing till I saw his head whip around and stare at the kid—he was at the desk evidently asking where the men's room was. It hit me—I thought, my God, it's Dunlop. The kid started down the hall. I went after them and they both went into the men's room—it was around a corner and kind of out of the way. I waited at a phone slot—that's when I called you—and some guys and little kids come out laughing and then they were in there alone for a few seconds and then I hear a shot and Santa comes dashing out and takes off down the hall yelling, 'Help! Murder!' and so forth and I go in and the kid is lying across the toilet, frisked—the cash is gone—and dead. So what do I do? I come running out myself yelling the same thing and now Dunlop sees me and tries to get to me but there's confusion and people are dragging on him and kids are crying and I make the elevator first and pray that the door closes and it does." Dan looked over his shoulder. "It's a cinch he'll be up on the next one he can get."

We were halfway down the corridor and the service elevator sign gleamed red at the end. Both our heads seemed permanently fixed in a backward position. I gasped, "Dan, why did he have to kill that boy?"

"Oh, the kid undoubtedly put up a fight for the letter." His eyes still on the end of the hall, he took a long, dirty envelope from his pocket. "Take a quick look at this. I have to admit I'm curious."

So was I, but I looked at the thing with revulsion as Dan pounded on the DOWN button. Since nothing more sinister than a procession of supper trays was approaching us, I swallowed distaste and took from the envelope several sheets of paper. No need for in-depth perusal; it was a blurry string of accusations, recriminations, and exclamation points. I raced through the contents and said, "Listen to the postscript. 'I told him on the phone that his "wife's" shop was only a few blocks from St. Victor's Hospital, where my first husband died, and that whenever I was in the area I went to the chapel there to say a prayer for Lewis and for him. Isn't it pathetic of me, Clara, to still love him?' "

Dan and I looked at each other, he in exasperation, I in sorrow. Oh, let him be older—or a woman. Then he said, with another slam at the button, "We'll need a cab and there probably aren't any where this elevator arrives. You may be in for a chilly ride. Damn you, *come*!" This to the elevator. "You too, Sister, 'cause we ain't waitin' for you."

And at that moment she rounded the corner, being helped into her coat by Santa Claus.

I stuffed the letter back in my pocketbook and dragged my eyes to the elevator light. Dan must have done the same because he breathed to the door, "Now!"

Sister called gaily, "You wouldn't have wanted to miss *this* visitor! He made a trip up just to see you!"

The elevator pinged, and the door opened. Dan shoved me in and pushed the button, but Santa's red arm shot out and stopped the door.

"After you, Sister." He was chuckling. "Yes, this lady is a friend of mine, and I'm going to have some fun making her guess who I am."

"Can you give her a hint, Santa?" Sister looked at me merrily as the elevator started to descend. "And incidentally, you make a great St. Nick, doesn't he?"

"Yes, he does." I wasn't going to terrify or endanger this woman. "Let me think . . . the voice is familiar . . ." I looked up into the eyes of this terrible man, and they twinkled back at me over the snowy beard. "Have I known you long, Santa?"

"Long enough to know me well." It was said almost quietly and chilled me.

I said, "This is my friend, Dan Schenck."

Dan said, "Sorry I can't shake hands." He thumped his cast on the handle of the chair. "I broke my wrist the other day. I was mugged."

Sister looked shocked. "I didn't know that's how it happened, Mr. Schenck! You know, sometimes I'm positively ashamed of New York." The elevator stopped, the door opened, and there was a blast of wind and snow, and the sight of police cars, lights flashing through the early dusk. Sister continued her lament. "Will you look at this? What on earth do you suppose that accident could have been?"

Dan pushed me clear of the elevator, and I said, "Sister, I won't have you come a step farther. I have two fine escorts. Please go back to your floor."

"But somebody should—we're supposed to—" the poor thing was shivering, torn between duty and the temperature "—and your car must be way around—"

Dan said, "We're taking a cab. Maybe Santa will be kind enough to round one up."

My heart leaped. How could he refuse to go in search of one with Sister present? If I could just keep her still debating ... But Dunlop's voice was jovial and firm. "No way are you taking a cab. My car is right over there. I parked around back on purpose so the kids wouldn't see me get out. Mrs. Gamadge is right, Sister. We'll take good care of her." He reached for my pocketbook and bag. "Here, give me those."

But I clung to them and he didn't dare wrestle with me in the nun's presence. She was still hesitating. I said hopelessly, "Please go, Sister, and thanks again for everything."

I held out my hand to her and felt something separate from my wet palm. It fell to the ground, and Sister picked it up. She said delightedly, "A scapular!"

I was motionless. Dan was motionless. The only moving thing seemed to be the snow. Dunlop said politely, "What's a scapular?"

"Something like a medal, you might say." Sister examined it smiling. "People don't wear them much anymore. St. Benedict! I haven't seen a St. Benedict scapular in years!"

I said, cold to the bone, "It belonged to a friend of mine who died. Please keep it, Sister."

164

"Oh, but I shouldn't—"

"Really—it should go to someone who will appreciate it."

She looked up beaming. "Then it shall go to another saint—St. Nicholas!" She stood on tiptoe and hung it about Dunlop's neck. "There! St. Benedict will bless you for bringing joy to children. Good-bye."

She stepped back into the elevator, and the door closed. I looked at Dunlop incensed. I said, "Give me that!"

"We'll swap. Give me the letter."

"How dare you let that thing touch you!" My teeth were chattering. "You know who it belonged to!"

"Of course I do. She never took it off."

Dan said, "Mrs. Gamadge doesn't have the letter. I do."

Dunlop looked from one to the other of us. "I don't believe you."

Dan shrugged. "That's your problem. And what a shame. You've disposed of your perfectly good mugger. You'll have to take it yourself."

"I intend to." Dunlop scanned the lot through the driving snow, then he moved a few steps, his hands in his roomy, fur-trimmed pockets. "I don't have to tell you that this costume is a great place to stash a weapon. Just wheel the lady over to that blue Dodge, and we'll hop in. You can give me the letter then or on the road. Rotten day for a drive, but if you insist."

Dan said, "We're not budging."

"Yes, we are, Dan. I'm cold." I stood up. "Push the

chair up against the wall." I was shaking with rage and fright. "Now, let me hang on to you."

Dunlop attempted to support my other side but I pushed him away and clung to Dan, hobbling through the wet snow. The wind was icy but not as icy as my heart. I looked up at the tall figure walking beside me, the image of the saint reposing on his flowing beard. Obscene. He caught my glance, touched the thing smilingly, and said, "I told you—you can have it."

It was maddening to see police cars everywhere. There were honks as drivers waved to Santa and he waved back. I was afraid Dan might risk a break, and the same thought must have occurred to Dunlop. He said, "Don't try anything, Schenck. It would be a shame if Clara didn't get home for Christmas. Here we are. Put her in the front seat."

He stood, one hand still in his pocket, brushing snow from the windshield. Dan deposited me groaning on the seat, said, "Watch that leg," and lifted it gently in, leaning over me as he did so. He whispered, "Redmond's here."

He closed the door on my gasp, and Dunlop motioned him into the back. As Dunlop circled the car, I managed *"Where?"*

"Directly across from us. Look anywhere else."

"How? How?"

"License plate probably."

Dunlop climbed in, started the car, and set the windshield wipers going. He said, "Keep your one good hand to yourself, Schenck, because I also have a good hand. It's in my right pocket snuggled up real close to

Clara. Darn it, this thing scratches." With his left hand he pulled off the beard and, glancing at me with a smile, he adjusted the scapular carefully on his chest. "Now"—he put his headlights on—"where shall Santa take you for a ride? I hope it doesn't have to be all the way to the North Pole." He moved forward slowly. "Is anybody hungry besides me? Let's do the first drive-in. My treat. After all, 'tis the season to be—"

He broke off and leaned forward over the wheel, peering through the slushy windshield. The lights on the car across from us had gone on, and it was edging toward us. More headlights were flooding in through the rear window. Dunlop cursed and twisted the wheel violently to the left. As the car lurched, I heard him gag—suddenly, horribly—and his head pitched forward and struck the horn, one half of the scapular cord caught in the wheel, the other half tight around his neck. Like a flash Dan's good arm went out. He dragged Dunlop's head back against the seat and with his cast pinned the man's right hand to his side.

The image of St. Benedict dangled below the outraged, purpling face.

20

"SHADES OF ISADORA DUNCAN!"

Sadd put two-year-old Andrea on the floor, brushed crumbs from his lap, and poked the fire.

I said, "But Isadora didn't deserve it, poor thing."

Sadd and I had spent all of Christmas day—Sadd, in fact, all of Christmas Eve—asleep, staggering up only for a brief, mandatory appearance for exchange of presents that morning. Now it was late in the afternoon, and the young people were off skating along with Loretta Vaughan, who declared she'd won a medal for figure skating at the Fairfield Country Club in 1940.

Andrea had been wished upon us.

Only one survivor of the wreck had as yet been unable to face the day. Sal lay upstairs in a mercifully drugged sleep. It would be a while, her doctor had said, but this was a very strong woman. . . .

Andrea whined to be taken back on Sadd's lap, but he crossed his legs and said, "No, child, that's the end of my avuncular act. Go to your grandmother."

Andrea tottered toward the Christmas tree, and I put out a deterring hand. She batted it and trotted back toward the fire. Sadd's foot went up before her, and she yelled. I pulled her onto my lap, and she writhed down. Sadd pushed a toy to her, and she kicked it. He stood up. "Where did you get this child, Clara? In an army and navy store?" He took her hand. "Come help me mix another drink."

She trotted happily with him to the dry bar. The living room of Nice Ugly was a shambles, a wonderful après-Christmas shambles. I sat on the sofa with my leg propped up, the horror beginning to melt in the blessed glow of the fire.

Sadd said, "So was it the license plate?"

"That, plus the note Liza taped over her buzzer. The police took it with them."

"But how did they know you were making such an unorthodox departure from the hospital?"

"It seems Captain Redmond phoned my room just as Dan was whisking me away. A nurse told him I was on my way down and via what route."

Sadd had dumped a package of colorful cocktail straws on the rug, and Andrea was plopped beside them, entranced. I smiled as I looked at the expensive toys scattered about the room. Now he came back to his chair, gave me my drink, and sat down stretching.

I said, "Hasn't Loretta Vaughan been a terrific sport?"

"Why shouldn't she be?"

"Well, after all, there was a deception—"

"It was Janet Folsom's, you said, not the girl's— what's her name?"

"Liza."

"Now, there's an example of the resiliency of youth. Devastated as she is by all this, she's still able to at least join the skating party."

"Yes," I said, perhaps wistfully, "the resiliency of youth."

"Do you ever long to be young again, Clara?"

"Good Lord, no."

"Me neither. No, actually, that should be 'Nor do I.'"

We sat in silence, companionably old. The clock on the mantel, an antique carriage repeater that had belonged to Aunt Robbie and which Henry had begged for, struck five. The kids would be home soon. I stood up.

"I'm going up to check on Sal. Oh, dammit, Sadd, she just didn't deserve this."

"Well, there you touch on a subject that will baffle us all till Doomsday—the pain and suffering that's everyone's lot." He poked the fire, and it blazed up beautifully. "By way of consolation I can only remind you of the inspired words of that great sixteenth-century saint, Camillus De Lellis."

"What were they?"

"Nobody gets a free ride."

CLARA GAMADGE MYSTERIES
BY ELEANOR BOYLAN